Mist and Magic

A Death Before Dragons story

by Lindsay Buroker

Copyright © Lindsay Buroker 2020

No part of this book may be reproduced, scanned, or distributed in any printed or electronic form without permission. Please do not participate in or encourage piracy of copyrighted materials in violation of the author's rights. Thank you for respecting the hard work of this author.

This is a work of fiction. Names, characters, places, and incidents either are the product of the author's imagination or are used fictitiously, and any resemblance to locales, events, business establishments, or actual persons—living or dead—is entirely coincidental.

MIST AND MAGIC

LINDSAY BUROKER

CHAPTER 1

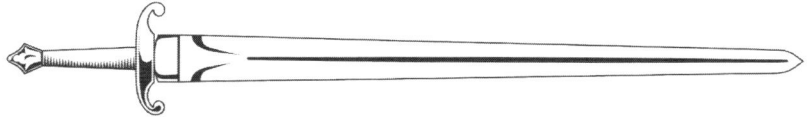

THE AUTUMNT FOG WAS SO thick that I almost stepped on the body sprawled across the dock before I saw it. The extremely *large* body. Leathery skin, yarn-like yellow hair, a club still gripped in his sausage fingers. Ogre.

Worry for the friend I'd come to check on churned in my gut, but I tamped down the emotions and groped for professional detachment. I was an assassin and killed bad guys for a living. This wasn't the first corpse I'd seen. It wasn't even the first corpse I'd seen this week.

"No big deal," I reassured myself.

Except it *was* the first corpse I'd seen located twenty feet from the boat my best friend lived aboard.

"Michael," I murmured, drawing Fezzik—my magically-enhanced compact submachine pistol—from my thigh holster, "what have you gotten yourself into?"

I listened for voices or anything out of the ordinary as I scanned the area, searching for whoever had killed the ogre. But the dense fog muted the lights along the docks, leaving hundreds of shadows—hundreds of hiding spots.

Beyond the breakwater, Puget Sound lay quiet, and waves barely lapped against the boats in the marina. If anyone had been stirring nearby, I would have heard them.

My sixth sense told me more than my eyes or ears. Thanks to my half-elven blood, I could detect magical artifacts as well as the auras of magical beings. The ogre didn't register, so I knew he was dead without checking for a pulse, but something at the end of the dock where Michael's boat was moored tickled my senses. The various enchanted trinkets he'd found during his years as a treasure hunter were familiar, but there was something else. Something alive inside.

It wasn't Michael. He was a full-blooded mundane human and didn't have a detectable aura. This was something else, something I'd never encountered before.

I wanted to investigate, but I opened my phone's flashlight app to check the body first. As much as I worried about my friend—corpses at one's front door were rarely a good omen—I didn't want to barge into what was likely trouble without knowing as much as I could.

The ogre had died on his back, and I didn't see any knife wounds or bullet holes on his torso or neck, but blood had seeped out from under his back and darkened the dock. I crouched and touched it. The blood had chilled but not yet dried. This hadn't happened long ago.

I holstered Fezzik and set my phone aside as I wondered if I could roll the nine-foot-tall ogre over to look at his back. My elven heritage gave me more strength than the average woman, and my six feet in height gave me long arms to use as levers, but ogres were typically three hundred pounds or more. And this guy didn't look like he'd been on a diet.

Careful not to grunt or make noise, I gripped the ogre's shaggy yellow hair and lifted his head, then crouched to use my legs and heave at the shoulder. My muscles strained, but his torso lifted off the ground.

A clunk and scrape came from underneath the ogre. Bracing him with my body so he didn't thump back down, I grabbed my phone and shined the light under him. The dock was drenched in blood, but I didn't see what had made the clunk until I lifted the light to the ogre's back. The long wooden handle of a kama knife stuck out of it, the curving sickle-like blade sunken deep.

It was one of Michael's weapons. I bit my lip, debating if I should remove it, lest it be used to identify him as the killer. It wasn't like the Seattle PD—or any police department in the world—acknowledged that magical beings took refuge on Earth or worried about justice for them, but there were clans of ogres around the city who might come to avenge their fallen brother.

I wiggled the weapon out. I had little doubt that Michael had been defending himself, but if there hadn't been any witnesses—and even if there had been—it would be hard to reason with irate ogres.

Stepping back, I let the body thump back down. An urge to protect my friend came over me, even though I didn't yet know what this was about, and I was tempted to roll it into the water so nobody would find it.

"Better talk to Michael first," I whispered, pulling out the rag I used to clean my other weapon—a magical longsword I'd dubbed Chopper—to wipe down his kama before tucking it in my belt.

I jumped past the ogre and continued to the boat. As I was about to hop onto the gangplank, footsteps thudded on the other end of the dock. Running footsteps coming from the parking lot.

Grimacing, I hoped an enemy approached instead of the person who'd called earlier and asked me to meet her down here. There hadn't been time yet to figure out what had happened.

A figure came into view, gray and indistinct in the fog. A flashlight beam punctured the mist, moving around like a lightsaber as the person ran.

"Julie?" I crouched and gripped Fezzik in case it wasn't.

The figure halted. "Val?"

"Yeah." I lowered my firearm. "Be careful. There's a dead ogre on the dock."

"A what? Is Michael okay?"

"An ogre. And I'm not sure yet. I don't think he's here." If he *was* here, he might be unconscious or dead. It was hard to imagine him leaving his weapon in the back of a fallen enemy and going to bed.

Julie Kwon came closer, gingerly maneuvering around the ogre. Her dyed blonde hair stood out now that she was a few steps away.

"Where else could he be?" Julie stared at me, her dark eyes wide. "He hasn't come to visit the family for more than a week. When we asked him to come to dinner yesterday, he said he'd found the clue of a lifetime and couldn't make it. Now today, he's not answering his phone at all. I'm afraid he's gotten himself in trouble." Her tone turned anguished when she added, "*Again.*"

Her lips pressed together tightly as she looked from my combat boots to the pistol in my hand to my belt filled with ammo pouches to my black leather duster jacket. The blonde braid dangling over my shoulder was my only nod to femininity, at least when I was working.

I braced myself for Julie to add that Michael had never gotten into trouble or known about the magical world until he'd met *me*. I never knew what to say to that. It *was* because of me—because of a mission Michael had followed me on where we'd chanced across an ancient dwarven text about relics—that he'd learned of priceless artifacts brought to Earth over the centuries by magical visitors and refugees. But it wasn't as if I'd told him to turn away from his finance job to become a treasure hunter. I'd specifically told him *not* to do that. Numerous times. When mundane humans got involved with magical beings, it rarely went well.

"You never should have given him that book," Julie said, as if she were reading my mind. But she was as human as Michael and had no telepathic powers. Blaming me was just what she did.

"I didn't *give* it to him. He found it when he was with me."

"You could have taken it from him. You're a damn ex-military thug. I know you could have."

I didn't point out that Michael was ex-military too—that was how I'd met him—since I knew what she meant. Michael had been a financial-management technician, and I'd been dragged away from my pilot MOS as soon as the army found out I healed five times faster than a regular human. The special training and missions that had ensued meant Julie was right. I was a professional thug.

"I'm checking on him," Julie said, waving away whatever further criticisms she wanted to fling.

It wasn't as if I hadn't heard them all before. But this time, with Michael in trouble, they stung more than usual. The truth always hurt.

I caught Julie before she could step on the gangplank. "There's someone or something magical inside. *I'll* check on him."

"Fine." She waved for me to go first.

I walked the short gangplank to the narrow deck of the boat. The *yacht*, Michael always insisted on calling it, but the one-room cabin with the bed in a glorified cabinet in the back did not inspire such lofty labels from me.

In the dark, I almost missed the blood splotches on the railing and deck. The ogre's blood, I hoped. Not Michael's.

I drew Fezzik and inched toward the door. Out at West Point, the foghorn blew, and I barely kept from jumping.

The cabin door was closed but not locked. I paused with my hand on the latch. The magical being I'd sensed inside was still there, and it had moved. Before, it had been near the front of the cabin, but now, it was in the back. Hiding in the cubby that held the bed?

The gangplank creaked behind me. Julie.

"Wait out here." I held up a hand. "Behind that post in case there's a firefight."

Julie hesitated, expression mulish for a moment, but she decided to obey. She climbed off the gangplank and crouched down behind the post.

I reached for a charm-filled leather thong around my neck and tapped a magical trinket that would camouflage me from sight, smell, and magical senses. I tugged the latch open, staying behind the door in case someone fired—or cast magic—out.

Nothing happened. The magical being didn't move.

After waiting a few seconds, I was about to head in, but I sensed something else. Out in the water, more magical beings came within range of my senses. Unlike the one in Michael's boat, these had familiar auras. There were several trolls and… I frowned with abrupt suspicion. An ogre.

They seemed to be on a boat out past the breakwater, but I couldn't make out its outline. If it had running lights, the fog was too dense for me to see them—or they had them turned off because they were hiding.

Was that where the ogre had come from? A boat that had come in close enough to deposit him, and perhaps others, to kidnap Michael? Or kill him?

"Are you inside?" Julie whispered loudly, unable to see me now that I'd activated my charm.

I rolled my eyes, wishing I'd warned her to stay quiet. This was why I never worked with a partner.

I resisted the urge to ignore her, since she might come to check if I did. "Checking now. Stay there and don't move or talk. There are trolls and another ogre out on a boat."

Though my charm should make it hard for anyone inside to see me, I still crept around the door in a low crouch with my finger on Fezzik's trigger.

It was dark inside, the only light coming from an alarm clock and a computer's power indicator, but that was enough to see that books and papers were strewn all over the floor. The decorative wooden navigation wheel that was usually mounted on the wall had been hurled into one of the portholes, one of the handles stuck through the shattered glass. Clothing had been pulled out from the built-in dresser and thrown in heaps. In the back, the bedding was rucked up in piles, blankets tangled around pillows.

I didn't see what I'd feared I would find: Michael's body.

But I still sensed the magical being. I didn't see anyone, but this close, there was no mistake.

I crept toward the open cupboard door of the bed nook—I refused to call it a bedroom since the mattress was the only thing inside. Once, I'd teased Michael for sleeping in something smaller than Harry Potter's cupboard under the stairs. He'd informed me that Harry hadn't had a view of Puget Sound and had pointed majestically at the tiny porthole that looked at the boat in the next slip, not the water.

The bed was empty. And there wasn't anything but a storage cabinet underneath it. Michael kept maintenance stuff for the boat under there. It was hard to imagine even a tiny child being able to fit, but I carefully opened the door. It was still stuffed full of maintenance equipment.

Maybe some magical beacon or trap had been left in the boat to fool my senses. Was that possible? I'd never encountered such a thing.

I risked turning on my flashlight app again in case I'd missed someone in the rumpled comforter on the mattress. Nope.

As I backed away, a high-pitched growl came from under the comforter.

A dog? A cat? Neither would explain the magical aura.

I pointed Fezzik at the lump. It moved slightly.

Using the muzzle of the pistol, I nudged the comforter aside.

A feline screech filled the cabin, and fearful green eyes stared straight at me. A large silver cat with black stripes sat amid the tangled bedding. This close, the creature would be able to see through the magic of my charm. It swiped at the comforter, as if it wanted to pull it back over itself. That paw was crazy large for a cat. And was the fur glowing faintly in the dark?

I put away the flashlight. Yes, there was a faint silver glow to the cat's fur.

"No, you're not a cat, are you?" I guessed him or her to be fifteen or twenty pounds with a lot of room to grow, if those paws were any indication. "Are you a tiger?"

I'd seen white tigers before. I hadn't seen silver tigers with glowing fur.

The cat—tiger cub—screeched at me and swiped a paw in the air but didn't look particularly threatening. I lowered my firearm and gazed around at the mess again, but there was nobody else inside.

"Where are you, Michael?"

The cub screeched again.

"And what am I supposed to do with this cat?"

CHAPTER 2

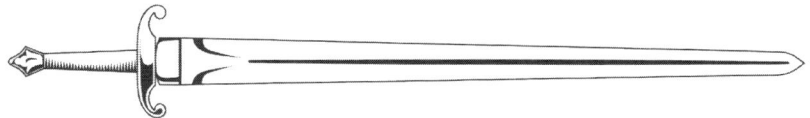

"THAT NOTEPAD ON THE TABLE is for you," Michael said. "Happy birthday."

"A notepad. I bet that's what you get all your girlfriends." Girlfriends. The word felt strange coming out of my mouth, maybe because I hadn't dated anyone since my divorce. Of course, Michael and I weren't officially dating, but we did talk about my assignments and his projects while eating and before having sex, so that probably fit some definition of the term somewhere.

"I do, but I only put a bow on it if I really care."

"And a ribbon with curlicues. Very fancy."

"It didn't come that way. I used a trick my mom showed me with scissors to make the ribbon curl."

"Some ancient family secret brought over from Korea, huh?"

"I'm pretty sure she got it off the Home and Garden channel."

Michael watched with a smirk as I slid the ribbon off and opened the notebook. We were inside his newly acquired yacht, as he called it, and he was giving me a tour. Had given me a tour. It had only taken ten seconds to see everything, including the composting toilet that I vowed never to use, and then he'd flopped down on the bed. The contents of the notebook were far more intriguing than that boat, especially when I flipped to a hand-drawn map and a bunch of instructions for finding The Secret Cave.

"The Secret Cave? That's not some rendezvous spot you want me to meet you at, is it?" It looked like it was over on the Olympic Peninsula. That was a long trip for a tryst.

"No. You said you needed to find the Kryftok Kobold Clan because they're harboring a fugitive you're supposed to take down. I had free time today, so I did some research for you. I've done a lot of treasure hunting over there, so I know the area well."

"You don't have to look up my marks for me." But I lowered the notepad, touched that he'd taken the time to do so.

"I know, but it's your birthday. Care to join me in the love nest for further celebrations?" Michael patted the comforter and gave me his version of bedroom eyes. An impressive feat given that he was reclining in a cupboard, not a bedroom, and that mattress was more suitable for a ten-year-old than a couple of amorous adults.

"Is that what the realtor who bilked you out of your life's savings called it?" I leaned my hip against the end of the table. It wobbled, threatening to fold down into the wall.

"Silly Val. You buy a boat from a boat trader, not a realtor."

"Are you sure you didn't get this from a police auction? It's named after a Russian submarine."

"The *Kursk*? How do you know?"

"I'm a crack researcher too."

"Does that mean you Googled it on your phone?"

I couldn't believe he hadn't. He was far better at finding things than I was. But maybe one didn't locate magical treasures by Googling them.

"That's how crack research is done these days," I informed him, deciding not to point out that the Russian sub had sunk, killing its entire crew. Whoever had named this boat had possessed an odd sense of humor. "You better check the nooks and crannies for leftover smuggled drugs."

Michael pushed a hand through his straight black hair. "Does all this vitriol for my new home mean I'm going to have to drive us back to your place if I want to get lucky tonight?"

"I don't know. You haven't taken off your shirt and rubbed your chest suggestively yet."

His eyebrows rose. "Would that work?"

"You do have a nice chest."

His lips curved into a smile, and he patted the bed again. "Ditto."

I snorted, certain I'd end up hitting my head on the wall—if not the ceiling—but he had *gotten me a gift. Besides, he was so proud of his new acquisition that I would feel bad rejecting it tonight.* Tomorrow, I would reject it.

The tiger cub screeched, pulling me from my memories. It was just as well. With potential enemies about, this wasn't the time to lose myself in the past.

"What's up, kid?" I asked absently, stretching out with my senses to see if the trolls and ogre had moved. They hadn't. If they were on a boat, they must have dropped anchor. "You thirsty? Hungry?"

The cub rolled onto its side and pawed at its ears. That gave me the opportunity to invade its privacy with my flashlight and learn that it was a female cub.

"Good. I don't have to call you an *it* now."

The next noise was a plaintive mew.

I grabbed one of Michael's two bowls—his personal bowl and his guest bowl, as he called them—from an overhead cabinet that hadn't been disturbed by the ransacking and filled it with water from the little sink.

"Here, kid." I put the bowl on the mattress where it—she—could reach it. The floor might have been better, but the cub seemed to like the bed, and I wasn't inclined to pick her up and move her. The claws weren't long yet, but they were there.

"Val?" Julie called, her tone almost as plaintive as the cub's. "What's going on?"

"I'm not sure yet, but you can come in."

I debated if I wanted to turn on the lights to do a better search. If the ogre—or ogres—had come from that boat out there, someone on it might be watching this spot. Though I couldn't imagine why. If they were the kidnappers, they already *had* Michael. I wished I knew why. To question him about some treasure he was hunting? To ransom him to his family? To *me*? If they knew how little money I had in my bank account, they wouldn't bother. Besides, we'd broken up almost a year earlier. Someone would have had to do a lot of research to link us together.

As Julie walked in, I flipped on the lights. I would risk it. There might be answers here in the mess.

The cub screeched a complaint.

Julie jumped, cracking her head on the low doorjamb. "What was that? Michael got a cat?"

"In a manner of speaking." I pointed her toward the bed while I picked up papers, looking through them as I stacked them on the table. Several had been ripped and crumpled, and a few were stamped with boot prints. *Giant* boot prints.

I couldn't tell if two ogres had been here, but that was my guess. Michael had gotten the best of one, but the other had gotten the best of him. And kidnapped him and carted him off. I hoped that was what had happened, not that he'd been killed and dumped overboard.

"That's a hella weird cat," Julie said. "It looks like a tiger cub. A white tiger cub? Do they start out darker and get lighter?"

"I don't know, but it's magical. *Very* magical." A burlap sack slumped in a corner caught my eye, and I picked it up.

"What does that mean?"

"It's not from Earth, at least not originally."

"Oh, I see. It's a Martian tiger."

I shook my head, having no interest in explaining the various worlds in the Cosmic Realms or that powerful magical beings could make portals and travel between them. It wasn't as if I was an expert. Everything I knew had come via trolls, goblins, orcs, and other beings that showed up here after fleeing trouble in their home worlds. Apparently, our populous planet was an excellent place to hide.

The burlap sack was empty save for a few short pale hairs—tiger fur?—and a crumpled note at the bottom.

"You don't think Michael *stole* it, do you?" Julie was eyeing the cub. "He wouldn't steal an animal. He's not hard up for money. Omma and Appa check on him. His investments do well, even if he's not making much of himself." She glowered at me, the suggestion hanging in the air that it was my fault.

More interested in the note than her speculations, I didn't answer. It had a scattering of symbols. Words?

I opened my phone's translator app, selected *detect language*, and pointed the camera at the note.

Unknown language, the app flashed.

"I figured that would be too easy."

"Val?" Julie faced me, now holding the cub to her chest. It was struggling and didn't look like it wanted to be held. "Do you know anything about this?"

"I know that's not a house cat and that you might not want to try to snuggle it."

"You know what I mean."

"I haven't talked to Michael for a couple of weeks and don't know what he's up to right now, no. But if he'd stolen the tiger and someone had come looking for her, you'd think they would have taken the tiger back, not him." I couldn't even imagine where one would steal a magical tiger cub *from*.

If I couldn't find any better clues, I was going to have to call Colonel Hobbs, the army officer who commanded a secret unit posted in an anonymous government building in Seattle. He and his soldiers quietly researched and dealt with magical beings that caused trouble in the Pacific Northwest. Hobbs had agents who did nothing but gather data and collate it into handy slide presentations for superior officers and government officials.

Up until a few months ago, Hobbs had hired me regularly for contract jobs, but for some reason, I hadn't heard from him lately. As my bank account keenly knew. Freelance gigs were few and far between, unless one was willing to branch out to assassinating humans, which I wasn't.

Hopefully, I hadn't been blacklisted for being a sarcastic smartass. Hobbs had tolerated my acerbic wit, since I was no longer active duty, but the army as a whole wasn't always into that.

"Ouch," Julie blurted and dropped the cub, flinging a hand to a cut on her jaw.

I dropped the sack and lunged, catching the cub an inch above the floor. Not wanting a swat of my own, I released her promptly. She'd twisted so she would have landed feet-first, as one would expect from a feline, but I wasn't sure how durable cubs were.

As soon as I released her, she darted away. I swore and lunged to shut the door—she and the note were my only clues right now—but she went to the sack and tried to burrow into it, kneading the burlap with her claws.

Julie lowered her hand, frowning at the blood on her fingers. "I'm going to try calling Michael again."

It wasn't clear if her reason was to see if he answered because she was concerned about him, or if she wanted to complain about the cub and her claws.

"Can you watch the cat for a minute?" I tucked the note in my pocket, intending to visit Hobbs to see if one of his people could translate it.

A phone rang, and Julie frowned at me. It took me a second to realize it wasn't her phone that was ringing.

She climbed across the mattress, stuck her hand between it and the wall, and pulled out a black phone. Michael's phone.

"Do you know the code to unlock it?" I asked. "Maybe he's got some voicemails or notes about what weird things he's been doing this week."

I eyed the cub. She had moved from kneading the sack to investigating the strings on one of my black combat boots. They *had* been tucked inside. Now, they were in danger of being shredded.

Julie tried a couple of guesses and shook her head. "Don't *you* know it? I'm just his sister, not his lover."

"We're not that anymore."

Something she ought to know, though maybe I was glad that he hadn't given her all the details. Not that it had been messy or mean. Just awkward. We'd managed to remain friends, but it had never been quite the same as before we'd started sleeping together. Life. Always complicated.

"No? He still talks about you a lot." Her lips twisted with distaste, and she looked dismissively down my form again.

"That's because I'm interesting. Watch the cub, please. I'm going to search the ogre for clues." And maybe figure out a way to get to the boat anchored outside of the breakwater.

The cub tried to follow me out of the cabin. Maybe she thought I could conjure up something more interesting than water.

"Cats are supposed to be independent," I told her, though I felt bad shutting the door in her face.

Earlier, I hadn't checked the ogre's pockets. I did so now, as well as patting him down for weapons beyond the obvious club. He had a dagger stuck through his belt—on a human, it would have been more like a sword—but no firearms, nor any magical artifacts that I could detect. I found a note in his pocket.

"What are the odds that you hold the cipher for decoding the other one?" I muttered, running my flashlight over it.

Three rows of large chicken scratches were all I got for an answer. They looked nothing like the symbols on the other note, and I was fairly certain I'd seen this language before. Ogre. I tried my translation app in case I was wrong, but once again, it did not recognize the words.

"Hobbs needs to get one of his people to make an app that detects trollish, elven, ogrish, and the like."

A grunt wafted over the water, my keener than average hearing picking it up over the lapping of waves. I also heard what sounded like oars dipping rhythmically into the water. My senses told me the ogre and a troll were heading to the marina.

I pocketed the ogre's note and drew Fezzik. It was time to get some answers.

CHAPTER 3

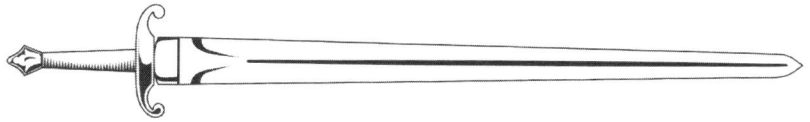

THE TROLL AND OGRE WERE cutting through the fog in a rowboat, as if this were 1820 and motors hadn't been invented yet. Maybe they didn't want to make any noise.

Before I could see them, my senses told me they were angling for another dock, not the one where Michael's boat was. That might mean they had nothing to do with him. It might also mean they couldn't see where they were going in the fog and planned to dock at the closest spot and then walk.

Why they would be coming back, I didn't know, but I had questions for them. I left Julie and the cub on the boat and trotted soundlessly back to land, then headed to the last dock that jutted out into the harbor.

A car was idling in the parking lot with its lights off. That almost made me pause, but neither of the men smoking inside, the red tips of their cigarettes visible in the dark, registered as magical to me. Right now, I was far more interested in ogres.

The rowboat was coming into an empty slip. I ran out on the dock, tapping my cloaking charm as I went. I also activated the charm dangling next to it, one that would translate anything they spoke in their native tongues into English. Too bad it didn't work on written text.

From this dock, I could make out the dark outline of a barge beyond the breakwater. The fog still shrouded it, but my senses told me it was where the other trolls were. As I'd suspected, they were running with their lights off. These guys were definitely up to no good.

The ogre clambered out of the rowboat first, the craft rocking wildly as his smaller companion cursed at him. Smaller was relative. The blue-skinned troll was more than seven feet tall with the shoulders of a defensive lineman.

Because he was lifting a box out of the boat, the ogre had his back to me. I swapped my firearm for my sword and glided in to rest the blade against the back of his neck while his hands were full. The side of his neck against his jugular would have been better, but he was too tall for me to reach that without standing on a stepladder.

The ogre dropped the box and started to turn, but I pressed the tip of my sword in and drew blood. Chopper's blade always glowed a faint blue, but it flared brighter at the promise of battle.

The ogre froze, and the troll lunged to his feet, spotting me through the magic of my charm. But even if he had a weapon, I'd placed myself fully behind the ogre.

"Don't," I warned him, then addressed both. "What did you idiots do with Michael Kwon?"

Most magical beings who took refuge on Earth learned enough of the local language to get by, but the ogre only cursed again and barked, "Who the fuck are you?" in his native language.

No, I realized as my brain caught up to what I was hearing and what my charm was translating. That was Russian, not ogrish.

"It's a woman," the troll said—*he* was speaking in his native tongue. "With a sword."

"No shit," the ogre said, switching to the troll language. These guys could be translators for the UN if they turned their efforts to good instead of evil.

"Where's Michael Kwon?" I repeated, though I was starting to fear they didn't understand English. If they'd come over from Russia, that would make sense.

The ogre spun. Before I could decide if I wanted to cut him further and risk killing him, he lunged and threw a punch at me.

I had some of my elven father's agility and dodged the powerful blow. A good thing because an ogre punch could knock a person's head off.

He snarled and drew a knife. I swept Chopper up to defend against a stab, annoyed with myself for hesitating and letting him take the offensive. But I hadn't come to kill these guys, just talk to them. Unless the bastards had killed Michael. Then all bets were off.

The clangs of our blades meeting rang out in the night, though the mist muffled the sounds. He pressed me back, trying to angle me off the dock on the far side, but I danced away, not letting him trap me.

He was stronger than I was but slower, and it wasn't difficult to evade his reach. Getting past those long arms and close enough to strike a blow was another matter. When his arm was extended toward the end of an angry slash at my head, I ducked and flowed under his arm. Chopper sliced through his leather jerkin and cut into his side as I ran past.

The ogre roared, spun, and flung himself at me like a sumo wrestler. His rage gave him speed, and I barely escaped his grasp as he smashed chest-first to the dock. Sturdy cement pilings shuddered, and it felt like an earthquake. Had I been caught under him, he would have crushed every one of my ribs.

Before he could rise, I rushed in and jabbed Chopper's point into the side of his neck.

"Stop," I growled, keeping myself from digging in too deep. "I just want to question you."

"Fuck you," he snarled in Russian and grabbed for my foot, determined to pull me down with him.

I jumped over the grasping hand. I might have leaped away again, but with the ogre flat on his belly, the troll in the rowboat had a clear line of fire at me now. He hefted a Dragunov sniper rifle with both arms and took aim at me.

These guys did *not* want to talk.

I slashed into the back of the ogre's neck, knowing I couldn't trade blows with him when the troll was shooting at me, then dove and rolled across the hard dock a split second before the troll fired. As I rolled, I yanked out Fezzik. Bullets sprayed the air where I'd been and cracked against the breakwater beyond the docks.

Coming up on one knee, I fired three times at the troll, magical rounds leaving a blue trail in the air as they slammed into his chest.

Even from my knees, my aim was true. The Russian rifle tumbled out of the troll's hands as he pitched backward, almost falling out of the rowboat.

Tires squealed in the parking lot, startling me until I remembered the two men in the car. Had they been contacts here to meet the troll and ogre?

The car peeled through the fog toward the marina exit. I sprang to my feet, but there was no way I would catch it.

Or so I thought. Sirens wailed and police lights flashed to life. Unmarked cars drove in, heading off the vehicle attempting to flee. Tires squealed again as the civilian car wheeled and roared deeper into the lot. I gaped as the police cars chased after it.

What the hell had I stumbled into? Or what had *Michael* stumbled into?

I thought about disappearing, but I'd helped the police numerous times with magical criminals they didn't have the resources to capture, so they should believe me if I told them I had acted in self-defense. And I had—sort of. I felt a twinge of guilt since I'd started the confrontation by threatening the ogre with my sword, but it was clear they were involved in something criminal.

The fleeing car crashed into a parked car. Its doors sprang open, and the two men raced out.

Between the fog and the distance, I didn't have a shot at seeing their faces, but the police were sure they wanted them. More car doors opened, and uniformed officers raced after them as the two men sprinted toward the buildings of the marina. One policeman shouted the customary *Stop. Seattle police*, but to no avail.

Curious about what was in the box, I climbed into the rowboat to take a peek. If it held another note in a language I couldn't read, I would kick it overboard.

Instead, it was full of dozens and dozens of small round cans, tunafish sized, stacked twelve deep and surrounded by dry ice. They weren't labeled, but I pried one open. Then wrinkled my nose at the fishy scent.

"Fish eggs? Caviar?" I poked my finger into one in disbelief, then shined my flashlight onto the little black eggs to verify that I wasn't wrong.

There had to be fifty pounds of the stuff in the box. My stomach started to sink as I realized this had to be some kind of smuggling operation. It was probably good that I'd helped stop it, but I seriously doubted this was the kind of thing Michael would be wrapped up in.

Gunshots fired over by the buildings. Another police car rolled toward the dock I was on and stopped.

The thought of disappearing popped into my mind again, but there were probably cameras around that had caught the fight, so I walked out to talk to them. Maybe they would trade information with me.

A male and female officer got out of the car as I stepped onto land.

"Ma'am." The woman held up a hand. "We've got an arrest in progress. We need you to go back to your boat."

They looked me over but didn't see my weapons. Both the sword—which I'd won in a battle with a zombie lord—and the gun—which a weapons-crafter acquaintance had made—were enchanted so that mundane humans didn't see them as long as they were on my person. I could remove them and show them off, but I rarely did.

"Caviar smugglers?" I asked.

"Yes." She glanced at her partner in surprise. "Beluga. It's illegal to harvest and import."

"The smugglers left their fishy booty on a rowboat back there." I tilted my thumb over my shoulder; the fog hid the bodies. "And there's a barge out past the breakwater." Or there had been. My senses told me those other trolls, and presumably the barge they came on, were moving off now. "I stumbled onto a troll and an ogre bringing the caviar in." I showed her the tin. "But I'm actually looking for a friend, Michael Kwon. We may need to file a missing-persons report. His sister is out on his boat."

The officer started to tell me that they could help once they were done, but a call for backup came in over their radio. They jumped into their car and raced over to where the others had parked, lights still flashing.

They hadn't taken the tin from me. What was I supposed to do with illegal fish eggs?

The trolls on the barge sailed out of range of my senses. I hoped I wasn't wrong about Michael's involvement in this and that he wasn't a prisoner on that barge, because I doubted the police would ever find it.

"Shit," I said as disappointment settled over me like a cloak.

Because my work was so dangerous, I avoided making new friends, and after years of ignoring old friends, I didn't have that many of them either. I didn't want to lose one of the few I had left.

I sensed a magical being approaching before the plaintive "merow" sounded. The cub padded toward me, still glowing a faint silver.

"Did Julie let you out, or are you an escape artist?"

She issued another sad sound.

It was probably a crime that came with a fine and up to ten years in jail, but I was feeling peevish, so I set the caviar tin down on the ground for the cub. I had no idea if she was old enough for solid foods or was missing her mother's milk. Did silver tigers from other worlds drink mother's milk?

The cub came forward and sniffed the tin, but she only sat in front of it and looked up at me with sad green eyes.

"That's my opinion of it too," I said, though it worried me that she wouldn't eat. Had she drunk any of the water in the boat? I hadn't seen her do so. "Hard to believe people would pay for it, much less risk their lives smuggling it."

The cub stood up and stuck her paw in the tin, then lifted it out, sniffed it, and shook it off. Some splattered my jeans.

"Thanks. I always wanted to carry around a thousand dollars in fish eggs on my pants."

Julie walked cautiously off the other dock as she glanced toward the police cars. She spotted me and ran over.

"How'd he get out?" She pointed at the cub.

"It's a she, and that was going to be my question for you."

"I don't know. You shut the door and he—she—was inside. I'm sure of it. I called my parents to let them know we hadn't found Michael, and when I turned around, the door was open and she was gone." Julie stared down at the cub. "Tigers can't open doors, right?"

I shrugged. "Maybe magical tigers can."

"What are you going to do with her? You can't take a tiger to the Humane Society."

"What am *I* going to do with her?" The cub swatted more caviar out of the tin. I was on the verge of pointing out that Michael was Julie's brother and that her family had a house with a yard—the landlord of my one-bedroom apartment didn't even allow dogs—but what did the Kwons know about taking care of magical animals? Michael's parents ran an office-supply store. "Take her with me, I guess."

"With you, where? Are you going to find Michael?"

"I have to." I didn't admit that Michael was not only one of my few friends but still the person I trusted the most—Julie would probably call that pathetic. I pulled the two notes out of my pocket. "As to where I'm going, first thing in the morning, I'm going to find someone who can translate these notes."

And I would cross my fingers that the foreign scribblings held the secret to where Michael had been taken and weren't simply an ogre's grocery list.

CHAPTER 4

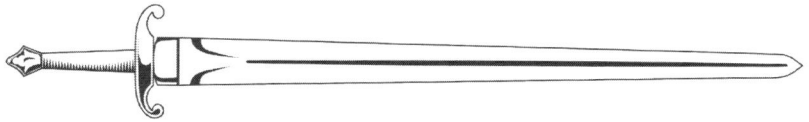

EARLY THE NEXT MORNING, AS I pulled up to the government building that held the offices for the army unit Colonel Hobbs commanded, I debated between taking the cub in with me or leaving her in the Jeep. In the scant hours I'd been home the night before, she'd shredded the end of my couch, destroyed my canvas grocery totes, torn the frame off the bathroom door, and left fang marks in three pairs of my boots. She was currently nibbling on the passenger-side seatbelt.

Since the Jeep was new and I'd barely started paying off the loan, I was disinclined to leave her loose inside. Besides, Colonel Hobbs or one of his people might know what world she came from and who could take care of her.

"Let's go for a walk, kid." I grabbed a backpack I'd selected for cat-carrying purposes and went around to the passenger-side door. The night before, I'd modified the opening so it was large enough for her head to stick out, and I'd lined the interior with the burlap sack that had been in Michael's boat. I opened the door, using my body to block it, and held the bag sideways so she could climb in. "Any chance you'll hop in here and we don't have to play games?"

She didn't try to spring past me and out of the car, but she did hold up a paw, her little brown claws on display.

"Is that a threat? Because I can take you to the dog groomer and have them trim those to nubs."

So far, she hadn't lashed out at me, but I remembered Julie's bloody chin and knew even domesticated cats could shred people's hands to avoid being stuffed into cat carriers.

The cub flopped onto her back, the pale silver fur of her belly exposed.

"I'm not sure if that means you give up or you want a belly rub. If you were my mom's golden retriever, I'd be positive it was the latter."

"Merow."

"That explains much, thanks."

A little wary, since all of those claw-filled paws were in the air now, I stroked the soft fur of her belly. She didn't object. The tail, which, like her feet, was too large for the current size of her body, spilled over the edge of the seat. After a few more strokes, I lifted the tail and scooted it and the rest of her body into the backpack. She allowed me to do it but promptly started nibbling on the edge.

"Just don't eat the bottom open while you're inside. From what I remember of this building, the floors are tile. Not cushy if you fall onto your butt on them."

"Merow."

"It's your call."

As I hefted the load onto my back and headed for the unmarked door to the army offices, it occurred to me that I'd become one of those people who had conversations with their pets. Too bad the cub didn't speak back in a language I could translate—out of curiosity, I'd already tried activating my charm—because I had a feeling she had seen what happened to Michael. And obviously, she had seen how she'd come to be on his boat in the first place.

"Need to find a telepath," I muttered.

If I couldn't get the notes translated, that would be my next step. A lot of the magical races had telepathic talents, though elves were the only ones I knew for certain could communicate with animals. Unfortunately, the elves and dwarves that had once had encampments on Earth had all left our world for reasons unknown shortly before I'd been born. According to my mother, my father had been among them, and he'd never returned. The odds of me meeting him or any other elf were low.

Since this army unit didn't officially exist, there wasn't an MP or any kind of guard to check my ID and decide if I was worthy enough to enter. That was good because I didn't have an appointment. It had been too late the night before to call, and it was probably still too early to do so.

At the first intersection, I hung a right and headed to Hobbs's office. When I'd worked with him in the past, I'd always found him in the building by seven or eight, so I anticipated him being there now. He had an outer office with an assistant I'd have to get past, but if it was the same lieutenant that had worked there before, he thought my boobs were pretty amazing and always passed me through after flirting with me.

But the outer office was empty when I reached it, the desk where the lieutenant had worked devoid of files or even a phone. Maybe Hobbs had gotten rid of his assistant.

I passed through and knocked on the metal frame of the door to his office. It was ajar, and I heard someone typing inside.

"What?" a woman inside asked.

Maybe Hobbs wasn't in yet after all or was doing something in another part of the building. If he'd gotten a new female assistant, she might be less interested in my boobs—and less likely to let me see her boss without an appointment.

"It's Val Thorvald. I'm looking for Hobbs." I pushed the door open.

A brown-skinned woman with hard eyes and short, wiry salt-and-pepper hair glared at me from behind a computer at the desk. She had a stocky build, a strong jaw, and a dyspeptic expression that immediately reminded me of the drill sergeant I'd had in Basic Training who'd called me Barbie and tormented me at every opportunity.

"*Colonel* Hobbs PCSed to Fort Bragg three months ago." Ugh, she even had the same Southern accent as my former drill-sergeant tormenter. "I trust there's no need to ask if you have an appointment."

"No, but I used to do work for him, and I was hoping for a favor."

"What kind of work?" She eyed my boots, jeans, and duster with the same disdain as Julie had. She didn't have any magical blood, so she didn't see my weapons, but her gaze snagged on the backpack. "And *what* is that?"

"I was hoping someone here would know, but I'm calling her a magical tiger for now." I turned so the cub's head was visible sticking out of the pack. In the bright office lighting, her silver glow was less noticeable, but her coloring alone ought to prove she was something unique. "I also need some notes translated."

"By all means." The woman—the name tag sewn on her chest said WILLARD, and her collar tabs denoted her a colonel in Military Intelligence—gestured expansively. "Come in, come in. We *love* to do research work for civilians who walk in off the street unannounced. And maybe I could get you some coffee while you're here. Cream? Sugar?" Her eyes narrowed. "*Lumps?*"

"I don't drink coffee." And I suspected she meant lumps on my head, delivered by a baseball bat, not lumps of sugar.

"I knew you were a heathen as soon as you walked in."

"Uh." Was that a joke? There was no humor in her eyes, nor did the corners of her mouth quirk upward. "I like sparkling water."

"How fabulous for you. What did you say your name was? Thorvald? Why does that sound familiar?" She turned to the computer, clicked the mouse a few times, and typed something in. Ignoring me utterly, she leaned back in her chair and started reading.

I had a feeling she was reading my military record and whatever notes Hobbs had left about me. It was also possible she wanted to know who was ranting about what political thing today on Facebook, but I doubted it.

Nibbling sounds came from behind my ear, and the cub shifted against my back. Getting into a better position to demolish the backpack, I imagined.

The phone rang.

"This is Colonel Willard," she answered.

A man on the other end spoke for quite a while. My hearing was better than average, but the nibbling sounds in my ear kept me from catching everything. I did pick out *Russian, trolls, smugglers,* and *caviar*. And finally, *Thorvald*.

"Funny," Willard said, eyeing me with open suspicion. "She just strolled into my office."

Something about her glare made me feel like I was in trouble. I shouldn't be. I'd stuck around the night before to tell the police what had happened, and they'd politely taken Julie's information on her missing brother. Since I had, however inadvertently, busted up what had been a handoff between smugglers and buyers, they hadn't been inclined to give me grief. As I'd suspected, none of them had been broken up over the deaths of the ogre and troll. Other ogres and trolls might learn that I had been responsible and take action against me, but the local law shouldn't.

"I'll have my people do some research and let you know what I can find out." Willard hung up, leaned back in her chair again, folded her arms over her chest, and stared at me. "Valmeyjar Thorvald, freelance assassin."

"Colonel Willard, occupier of Hobbs's desk."

I felt a little betrayed that Hobbs hadn't let me know he was leaving. We hadn't been close, but I'd done dozens of jobs for him in the years he'd been stationed here, and the army pay had allowed me to comfortably cover my bills and my apartment in Ballard. As in the rest of the Seattle area, the rent was a fortune, something I'd noticed even more since I hadn't had any of those army contracts lately.

"According to the police, you took it into your own hands to kill a troll and an ogre smuggler last night."

"I defended myself when they attacked me."

"You defended yourself with deadly force."

"It's a funny thing, but harmless force doesn't work real well on ogres." The smart part of my brain suggested that I shouldn't irk Willard, since she was potentially a source of work, but I didn't always listen to it. Besides, I had a feeling she'd already made her mind up about me and that ass-kissing wouldn't work. "Hobbs knew that. He used to hire me to handle things your mundane human agents couldn't."

"My mundane *human* agents are capable of handling a great deal."

"I'm strong, agile, quick, and I heal fast. I also have a giant magical sword that can cleave the balls off an irate ogre."

"Is that what you went to the docks to do last night?"

"Not until I found out that ogres were involved in my friend going missing. Any chance you have information on Michael Kwon?"

"No." Her mulish expression suggested she would never have information of any kind for me.

Damn it. I could do research on my own, but she had a whole staff of intelligence agents at her fingertips.

"He used to be in the army, and now he's missing." I tried to keep my tone reasonable. "The army's supposed to look after its own. Even if you don't want to help me, won't you help him? All I'm asking for is information you might hear about his disappearance. And to see if someone here can translate these notes."

I drew them from my pocket, opened them, and laid them on her desk. Maybe if she saw them, she would be intrigued.

Willard glanced at them and typed into her computer again. Michael's name.

"It's Korean," I said and spelled out, "K-W-O-N," to make sure she got it right.

"Thanks so much. I would have guessed it was the Ethiopian spelling."

"I'm here to help."

"Is that what you told the ogres when you arrived?"

"No." I clenched my jaw to keep from saying anything else, but I was one more snarky comment away from grabbing the notes and walking out. I didn't need this crap. Maybe Nin, the woman who'd crafted Fezzik, knew someone who could translate these languages.

"How long has Kwon been missing?" Willard grabbed the notes and walked out of the office.

I almost lunged after her to get them back, but the cub tugged on my braid with her teeth and distracted me.

"Not a toy," I grumbled, pulling it over my shoulder.

Fortunately, Willard was only going to a photocopier. She made copies of the notes and walked back into her office, pausing to look more closely at the cub.

"Not long," I said. "But there was a dead ogre on the dock, outside of his boat, and this little tiger inside. Since one of those smugglers was also an ogre, I thought they might be responsible." I *still* thought they might have been responsible.

"Do you always make assumptions based on race?"

"They're a species, not a race, and I make *suspicions* based on their proximity to the crime scene." I snatched the originals from her grip, annoyed at her insinuation, and annoyed that I wasn't making sense. Make suspicions? What did that even mean?

If I was honest with myself, I would agree that the previous night had not gone according to plan, and I could see why Willard would judge me for killing smugglers. Usually, when I took on jobs, it was to assassinate proven killers, magical beings who were not only hiding on Earth but preying on humans. Preying on beluga sturgeon didn't typically merit an assassination.

But I didn't want to be honest. I wanted to get out of here and find Michael.

"If you change your mind and want to be helpful, I'm sure Hobbs had my number." I headed for the door.

"Does that cat get any bigger?"

I paused. She was still looking at the cub, who was now swatting the back of my head with a paw, thankfully a paw with claws retracted.

"Bigger?"

"You said it's magical, right?"

"Yeah, I zap her with my sword, invoke the power of Grayskull, and she turns into a battle cat."

Willard snorted. "There *are* magical beings who can shift forms. Surely, you've encountered werewolves."

"Yes, but they don't go from mini wolves to giant wolves." I frowned at her. "Why do you ask?"

"There have been maulings up in Bellingham that have left three people dead. Six others have disappeared. I sent an agent up to investigate last week, and he stopped communicating with me two days ago." Willard tilted her head, still focused on the cub instead of me. "Nobody has seen the culprit, but the dead looked to have been killed by the claws of a giant feline."

If she'd been Hobbs and I hadn't been on my own mission, I would have offered to go up and find out what was going on. That was the kind of thing he'd paid me to do. But unless it was somehow tied in with this cub and Michael, I wasn't interested. Besides, it was obvious Willard would gnaw off her favorite limb before hiring me.

"This is the ogre language." Willard held up the note I'd taken out of the ogre's pocket.

"I know. I just can't read it."

"And this—" she held up the copy of the other one, "—is dragon."

"The dragon language? There haven't been any dragons on Earth for a thousand years." As far as I knew.

"Someone brought some of their words here. I also don't know what it says, but I recognize it. We've got translation dictionaries here. Lieutenant Reynolds is teaching himself the various magical languages. I'll have him look at these."

"And share the translations with me?"

She hesitated and glanced at the picture of Michael she'd pulled up with his file. "It'll depend on what they say."

I gritted my teeth. They were my notes, damn it. I had a right to know what they contained.

"See yourself out. I have a missing agent to find."

"A lot of people have gone missing lately," I observed.

"So it seems."

"You're going up to Bellingham?"

"If the creek don't rise."

It took me a moment to realize that was a Southern saying rather than a comment on the Skagit River or some other waterway between here and Bellingham.

"I could go with you to help if you want." I didn't want to, but if I helped her, maybe she would be more likely to share the results of the translations. Unfortunately, I didn't have any other leads at the moment. Besides, if I did some pro bono work for this new commander, maybe she would think of me for assignments later.

"I can handle it," Willard said tightly. "After looking over your record and your methods for obtaining results, I will officially say that this interview is over, and the army will not continue to employ you."

"I didn't come for an interview."

"You had one anyway."

"I wish you'd told me. I would have worn my dress jeans and brought my formal tiger."

Willard walked out of the office again. "See yourself out," she repeated over her shoulder.

"I suppose I shouldn't take you out of your pack and let you eat the furniture," I murmured to the cub.

"Merow."
"I still don't know what that means."
She swatted my braid.

CHAPTER 5

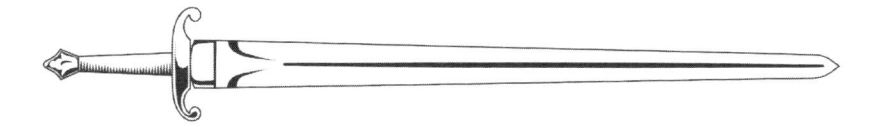

AFTER GRABBING A BURGER FROM a fast-food place, I drove to Shoreview Park next to Shoreline Community College and pulled in by the tennis courts. Unbeknownst to the students, staff, and legions of dog walkers, a clan of ogres lived in the woods between Boeing Creek and the Forest Loop Trail. Over the years, they'd burrowed out a cave, and one of their shamans had applied magical illusions to the area to keep mundane humans—and their mundane canines—from finding it. Now and then, dogs disappeared from the area, and the infrequently spotted coyote got blamed, but I knew better. Ogres thought dogs were legitimate snacks.

I grabbed both of my weapons as I climbed out of the Jeep, knowing I wouldn't be welcome. The reason I knew of the cave was because I'd had to drag a murderer out from the clan's midst a few years earlier. He'd been hauling off college kids and making stews with their choice body parts. The rest of the clan had claimed they hadn't known the source of the mystery meat, and Hobbs had only hired me to deal with the murderer himself, so that was all I'd done, but I'd had to fight off several of the others to get him and escape with my life.

Going back there was crazy, but I didn't know if Willard's agents would share the translations with me, and I needed someone who read ogrish. This was the only ogre hideout I knew about.

Earlier, I'd driven along the shoreline all the way from Lake Washington to Ballard, hoping to spot a suspicious barge out on the water—or sense the trolls from the night before—but that hadn't resulted in anything. I couldn't help but feel that I'd wasted most of the day.

In addition to my weapons, I grabbed a bag from Beast & Cleaver. It was full of cold cuts and ropes of sausage. My bribe for the ogres. I had some cash, too, but rumor had it, nine-foot-tall meat-eaters highly valued cold cuts and sausage.

It amazed me that the cub hadn't tried to devour the whole bag on the ride over. She'd sniffed it with interest but otherwise left it alone.

Raindrops spattered onto my head as I opened the passenger-side door. I caught the cub in the middle of gnawing on the seatbelt again.

"How come you chew on things, kid, but you don't eat anything?"

She looked at me and nibbled unrepentantly. I'd stopped her several times, but she'd still managed to get halfway through the belt. If I hadn't already offered her several kinds of food that day, I would have assumed she was hungry. But she'd turned her nose up at everything from the caviar to smoked salmon to cans of cat food to pieces of my burger.

"I should have left you in Willard's office. Just think what you'd do to computer cables."

The cub hopped down before I could stuff her in the backpack and ran across the parking lot.

Swearing, I grabbed the pack and hurried after her. Even if I wasn't convinced she needed me to take care of her, she was my only clue besides those notes, notes that might not say anything useful.

I chased her through puddles to the nearest patch of grass. Maybe she had to pee. I hadn't seen her drink yet, despite my attempts to give her water, so I had no idea how her magical metabolism worked, but maybe I was about to find out.

Instead of squatting, she flung herself on her back and rolled around, legs up in the air, paws twitching. A robin hunting for worms in a puddle flew off in an alarmed flutter. Another one watched the cub warily from the fallen leaves scattered under the bare branches of a tree.

"If you had an itch, you could have let me know." I stopped when it became apparent she wouldn't run farther. "I have dexterous hands."

She stood up, noticed the robin, and started stalking it, tail swishing behind her. The bird flew into the branches of the tree. The cub roared—sort of. It was on the thin and reedy side. The robin was unimpressed.

"I need to chat with some ogres. Are you coming, or do I need to put you in the bag?"

She turned, looked up at me, and roared again.

I walked away, curious if she would follow me. She did, but she took her time, sniffing every blade of grass and tramping through the puddles along the way. When I got far enough ahead that I thought I would have to go back to her, she sprinted to catch up and take the lead.

"An independent type, huh?" Given the reception I would likely get from the ogres, I wasn't sure I should take her along, but I worried that more than my seatbelts would be destroyed if I left her in the Jeep for an hour. She could demolish the entire interior in that time.

A blue jay squawked at us from a tree. The cub stopped again to roar at it. That only elicited more squawking.

"I'm sure your roar will drive fear into the hearts of your enemies someday," I said, "but you're not there yet."

The rain had picked up, and there were few walkers in the park, but someone yelled for me to put my dog on a leash. I waved, smiled, and ignored him. His face turned red, and he took out his phone and stalked off, no doubt to report me to the leash-enforcement authorities.

"What a sad world we live in that people can't recognize a magical tiger when they see one," I said, following my silver guide who through luck took the correct trail.

We tramped uphill into the trees, mud sucking at my boots. At least the dense evergreens kept some of the rain off my head.

I reached out with my senses, hoping to detect some ogres out and about, away from their cave. On my previous visit, I'd had a hard time finding it. The illusions not only kept humans away but camouflaged the auras of those inside.

"This way, kid," I called when I reached the spot where I'd gone off the trail before.

The cub was farther up, sniffing at a fern—no, she was *nibbling* at it—but she paused and looked at me. She seemed to debate something for a moment, then trotted over and sat by my legs.

"Do you understand me?" I wondered.

Green eyes gazed up at me. "Merow?"

"Hm."

She came with me as I left the trail, the mud and ferns and brambles difficult to navigate. The creek burbled past below, hidden by the undergrowth. Most of the time, I had a good sense of direction, but the slope and the forest terrain kept me from going in a straight line. I rolled my eyes and chided myself when I ended up coming back out on the trail. I veered off again, certain I wasn't far from the cave.

"I don't suppose you smell any ogres?" I still couldn't sense any, and I didn't see any giant prints. Here and there, humans and dogs had gone off the trail, leaving their tracks, but ogre prints would be much larger.

It was possible they were all staying inside because of the rain. It was also possible they'd moved their den after I'd found it and killed one of their kind.

I stopped, slumping against a tree trunk as I realized how possible that was. Or even *likely*.

Why had I assumed they would still be here? And what was my next move if they weren't? There was a basement pub in a building on Capitol Hill where magical beings gathered to drink and socialize. I was as welcome there as a fungus—and got shot at every time I went in—but maybe a few appropriately placed bribes there would give me a lead.

As I pushed away from the tree, ready to head back to the parking lot and try the pub, I swore. The cub had scampered off into the undergrowth. Though I had no doubt I could find her, I grimaced as I envisioned crawling under bushes and brambles to reach her.

Then I realized I no longer sensed her. My ability to detect magical beings extended about a mile, especially for a creature as magical as the cub, but she had disappeared. She couldn't have run a mile that quickly. No way.

A reedy roar came from somewhere nearby. What the hell? I could hear her but not sense her.

It dawned on me that she might have found the boundary of the ogres' magical illusion. Another roar sounded, this time with a tenuous wobble to it.

Afraid she was in trouble, I sprinted toward the noise, tree branches whipping at my face. I tapped my camouflage charm, realizing I might be about to burst in on a pack of ogres. One or two I could handle, but if their whole clan was home…

Magic nipped at my skin like fire ants as I passed through a barrier. The urge to flee in the other direction assaulted me, and I stumbled to a stop, fighting against my own legs. They wanted to obey that urge to flee.

I clenched my jaw and drew Chopper. The blade was capable of defeating the magical defenses of wizards and other enemies, but I'd also noticed it helped me resist magic that worked against my mind.

With the hilt cool in my grip, I willed the blade to drive away the compulsion to turn around. Control returned to me, and my legs carried me forward. The fire-ant feeling disappeared, and between one step and the next, my senses exploded with awareness of magical beings. A *lot* of magical beings.

CHAPTER 6

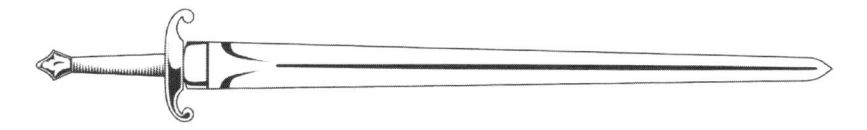

THE GOOD NEWS WAS THAT my wayward cub was visible at the mouth of a cave in the hillside up ahead. The bad news was that four ogres stood around her, two carrying clubs and two carrying swords. My senses told me there were more of them inside, beyond a curtain of dangling roots and moss.

The ogres were poorly nourished with pronounced cheekbones and their rough hide and burlap clothes dangling over gaunt frames. They might think a tiger cub was something good to eat.

Glad I'd thought to camouflage myself, I crept forward, willing my breathing to grow steady and quiet after my sprint through the woods. A bead of sweat dripped down the side of my face.

They spoke in their native tongue, and I tapped my translation charm.

"Where did it come from?" one of the club-wielders asked. "And how did it find us through the protection?"

"The cat is magical," another said with a grunt. "Trouble."

He bent to grab her by the scruff of her neck—or to wring her neck.

I rushed forward, sword raised, but the cub darted away before his fingers wrapped around her. She bounded into the cave and disappeared from sight. I stifled a groan. Why couldn't she have bounded *away* from the cave—and them?

Only ten steps from the group, I paused beside a tree and debated my options. They hadn't followed the cub inside, and I couldn't sneak past them. My camouflaging charm was powerful, but if I was within a few feet of someone, the effectiveness wore off.

A shout came from within the cave, followed by several curses. A thump followed, and I envisioned one of the brutish club-wielders slamming its weapon down on my poor cub.

Clenching my jaw, I strode forward. I couldn't fight this many ogres, but I couldn't let them kill the cub either. I would… think of something.

But before I reached the group, the cub bounded back out with a beheaded and plucked chicken in her mouth. The legs were still attached, and the yellow feet flopped on the ground as she ran.

All four of the ogres outside of the cave lunged for her. But the cub darted around their legs, and they ended up grabbing each other instead. One even cracked his head against another's head. It was like watching a cartoon.

The cub sped off into the woods. The ogres looked at each other, as if confused about whether they should give chase or let her go.

A female wearing a stained yellow apron and a bone ring in her nose stomped out with a meat cleaver and a kitchen spoon in her hands. "No, no, you boys relax. I'll go get the little thief."

Even through my translation charm, I could detect her sarcasm, but the male ogres pretended not to. They shrugged and went into the cave as the female strode in the direction the cub had gone.

Keeping my distance, I trailed quietly after her. This was my chance to talk to an ogre one on one. Was it possible the cub had intentionally lured her out for me? Or had she only wanted the chicken? So far, she had rejected all of my food offerings, but maybe plucked hens were the tiger's meow.

"Come here, you striped thief," the ogre growled, her meat cleaver raised overhead.

I grabbed a rock and, as she started to swing it downward, hurled it. My pistol would have been more effective, but the rest of the ogres would have heard the gunshots. The rock did the job as it slammed into the back of her wrist.

She let out a startled yelp, dropped the cleaver, and whirled toward me. Since I wasn't close enough for her to see through my charm's magic, she peered suspiciously about, scanning the trees.

"Who's playing with Big Mama?" she demanded.

Playing with? Ogres had rough games if they included rock hurling.

"Me." I moved several steps downhill, so the cave wouldn't be at my back, and tapped my charm to deactivate it.

The ogre swore, snatched up the meat cleaver, and waved it and the spoon menacingly at me.

I showed her Fezzik, in case she was thinking of stampeding me, but I didn't point the pistol at her. "That's my cub." Sort of. "I came to retrieve her. I don't want any trouble."

My charm only allowed me to understand others—it didn't translate my words into their language—so I didn't know if she understood me until she spoke.

She switched to English for my sake. "She stole my chicken."

The ferns near my feet rattled, and my muddy silver tiger cub scooted out from underneath the fronds. The chicken was now also muddy, but none of it had been devoured.

"You can have it back," I said as the ogre scrutinized me. I didn't remember her from my last visit, and I hoped she didn't remember me. "She just likes to mangle things, not eat them. And I'm willing to trade you a whole sack of meat if you can help me translate something. I was hoping to find an ogre back here who wouldn't mind doing the job."

"Help you?" Big Mama squinted at me. "You're the Ruin Bringer." That was one of the dubious monikers the magical community had for me. "You kill our kind."

"Only when your kind kills humans first. I'm not here to kill anyone today." Unless they were tied in with Michael's disappearance... but this one looked like a homebody, not a smuggler or kidnapper. "I want to make a fair trade for your time. It won't take long. I need a note written in your language translated."

"The Ruin Bringer isn't *fair* with ogres. You sent that thievin' varmint in to lure me out here."

Thievin' varmint? Apparently, they had a TV in that cave that was tuned to the all-Westerns channel.

"I'm fair with those who aren't criminals. Why don't you look at the note? If you can translate it, I'll pay you in meat or money. Your choice."

I hefted the bag of sausages I'd managed to keep ahold of during my sprint to the cave. "You have my word. I'm not a liar. I'm an honorable professional."

The cub flung the chicken onto my boots, grrred fiercely at it, then pounced on it. I sensed another ogre had left the cave, so I didn't look down, but I made a mental note to scrub my boots later.

"With a thievin' cat cub."

The chicken went sailing into the undergrowth, and the cub bounded after it. Something that looked suspiciously like a gizzard lay draped across my boot. I picked it up, put it in the bag of meat, then drew out the raw sausages to show the ogre.

"Lots of good food. Bratwurst, chorizo, applewood-smoked ham, salami. It can all be yours. If you can read, it'll only take a few seconds to look at the note."

"Of *course* Big Mama can read. The assumptions humans make about ogres, egads."

While I kept the pistol pointed at the ground in front of her, I pulled out the note. The male ogre was heading in this direction but taking a circuitous route. Either he didn't know exactly where Big Mama was, or he knew exactly where she was—and where I was—and was trying to sneak up behind me.

If not for my ability to sense magical beings, he might have been able to do so. Twilight was encroaching, making it difficult to pick things out between the trees.

"I want that chicken back," Big Mama said as I started toward her.

The cub was busy flinging the dead chicken about like a dog with a rope toy. By this point, it was hard to imagine anyone wanting it.

"*And* the meat." She eyed my bag and the sausage I'd left artfully dangling out to entice.

"How about you see if you can read my note first?"

"Chicken first, then I read, and then you give me the rest of the meat."

"Right." I sidled toward the cub. Even though we'd had a good relationship thus far, I wasn't positive she wouldn't try to eviscerate me—or more likely my feet—if I took her toy from her. If I thought she would eat the cold cuts, I would have traded her some salami for the maimed chicken.

Careful not to get my hand close to her claws, I darted in when she wasn't looking and grabbed the chicken. I hefted it up, only to find my twenty-pound cub attached to it, claws sunken in like fishhooks. I shook the chicken, hoping she would let go. She did not.

It was a challenge to keep my firearm pointed toward the ogre while I did all this, but I didn't dare let my guard down. Fortunately, Big Mama had crossed her meaty forearms over her chest and was waiting patiently.

The male ogre creeping closer was another matter. Just as I managed to tug the chicken away from the cub, who screeched like an annoyed Siamese, he stepped out from behind a tree with a weapon raised.

Without hesitating, I switched Fezzik to my other hand and pointed it between his eyes. At the same time, I scooted off to the side, so I could keep Big Mama in my peripheral vision.

Normally, I would have also drawn Chopper, so I could keep weapons pointed at both of them, but instead, I stood with my gun in one hand and a mangled and plucked chicken in the other. The Ruin Bringer indeed.

"My life has gotten weird since I met you, kid," I muttered to the cub.

Though I didn't take my focus from the ogres, I was aware of her trying to jump high enough to retrieve her prize.

Raising my voice, I said, "Stay put," to the newcomer.

I almost ordered him to drop his weapon, but it was a sling. Granted, an ogre sling held rocks the size of soccer balls and could take off my head, but I wasn't that worried about it.

"Big Mama is going to read something for me, and your clan is going to get a large and delicious dinner."

He looked at the mangled chicken and the cub trying to leap up and get it. Even though he didn't speak, he effectively oozed skepticism.

"She's got sausage," Big Mama said. "Give me the note, Ruin Bringer."

"Ruin Bringer!" the male blurted in their language. "You can't help her. She'll kill us all."

"She's got sausage," Big Mama repeated.

I was glad I'd thought to bring a food bribe rather than relying on money. It wasn't as if ogres could take wads of cash and walk into the delicatessen on their own. Magical refugees had to lie low and avoid humans, or they ended up being reported to people like me.

A twinge of sympathy went through me at the thought, but I remembered that ogres were behind Michael's disappearance and steeled myself toward these guys.

It took some effort to walk to Big Mama without tripping over the cub, but her order of operations seemed logical, so I handed her the chicken, then showed her the note. The cub finally gave up and flopped down on her side in the mud.

Big Mama stuck the chicken in an apron pocket large enough to hold half a pig and waved for me to hold the note higher. Her hands were grimy with guts and dirt.

"It's a human address," she said.

"Yes?" That sounded promising. If I hadn't been busy pointing my gun at the sullen ogre with the slingshot, I would have taken my phone out to type in whatever she told me.

"One Cave, Misty Loop Lane, Bellingham."

All roads led to Bellingham…

"One Cave? Is that the equivalent to a house number?"

"I can only say what is on the page, Ruin Bringer."

"Right." Disappointed the note hadn't contained more, I put it away and pulled out my phone to record the address, though I suspected I could remember that. "Did it say anything else?"

"No."

I tapped Misty Loop Lane Bellingham into my map and was surprised when a road came up. It was southeast of town, in the forested hills between Lake Whatcom and Highway 9, a meandering road that covered several miles. I added in One Cave, but a specific address failed to come up.

"The sausages," Big Mama said.

"Do you know if there's a clan of ogres up in Bellingham?"

"Ogres in lots of places."

I gave her the bag of meat in case that might help her remember specifics about Bellingham.

The male shambled toward us. My finger tightened on the trigger, but he'd lowered the slingshot. His focus was on the bag. I scooted back as he approached it and opened it with his finger.

"Smells goooood," he said, nostrils twitching.

Big Mama swatted his hand with the spoon when he tried to take off the sausage dangling on the outside.

"Not until dinner," she said, and stalked in the direction of their cave.

The male lingered and looked at me. I prepared to spring away in case he decided he needed to drive me away from their territory—or flatten me with a rock.

"Someone wanted to hire ogres a couple weeks back," he volunteered. "Someone who said there was work up north."

"Up north as in Bellingham?"

He rolled a broad shoulder. "Maybe. Human city names don't mean much to ogres."

"Any chance you saw who was doing the hiring?"

"I wasn't there, just heard about it from Zogg."

"Did Zogg take the job?"

"Nah. He said the guy was scary and dangerous and super powerful. Only a desperate fool would work for somebody like that." He shook his head, shaggy hair flopping about his shoulders. "But some ogres are desperate, so maybe they went. Nobody from our clan though. You got that?" He frowned at me. "Our clan doesn't make any trouble. Maybe you will forget this cave is here."

"Maybe I will," I agreed.

As he shambled away, I wondered what kind of being would be considered scary and dangerous to an ogre. They weren't afraid of much. They might call me the Ruin Bringer and be wary around me, but that wasn't the same as being scared.

CHAPTER 7

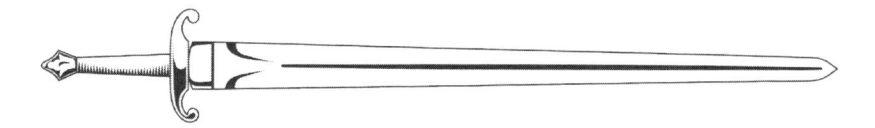

MY TIGER CUB HAD USED up all of her energy stealing and mercilessly pummeling the chicken, and she wouldn't be roused when I tried to coax her into walking back to the parking lot. I ended up carrying her to the trail and back down toward the tennis courts.

"I don't think this is normal," I informed her.

Her tired silver head flopped onto my shoulder. Her abrupt weariness surprised me, and I hoped it was because it was getting dark and she was naturally tired, not that something was wrong. It continued to concern me that she didn't eat or drink—how long could a cub go without food and water? Was it possible that if she was from another world, our food and water weren't sufficient for her needs?

That seemed unlikely. After all, the ogres were from another world and they wouldn't have any trouble hoovering those sausages.

"I wish I knew more about you, kid." I managed to shift her in my arms so I could open the Jeep door and put her on the seat. "You don't eat, you don't drink, and I haven't even seen you pee. I get that you're magical, but you're also a warm-blooded, furred… cat critter."

A sleepy green eye opened to consider me. "Merow?"

That sounded more wan than sleepy. I wanted to drive up to Bellingham to try to find this address, but I also wanted to find someone who knew what the cub was and could help her. Would a scary, dangerous guy who was hiring ogres be the answer?

"Sounds like more trouble to me." I closed the door, got in on the other side, and drove off, not toward Bellingham but toward the food truck that my weapons-making acquaintance ran in Pioneer Square.

During lunch and dinner hours, the proprietor Nin made a Thai beef-and-rice dish that was popular with people who worked in the area. After hours, she made magical weapons out of a nook in the back. They were popular with people who wanted to defend themselves from magical beings. Shifters, in particular, were strong enough to survive regular gunfire and bladed weapons, and I hadn't yet seen an ogre felled by a bullet that wasn't magical.

Nin had made Fezzik, and she replenished my ammo whenever I ran low. She also put together a mean magical grenade. I had a feeling I would need both up in Bellingham.

Since Nin was well versed in the magical—she'd been taught by her grandfather, a gnome tinkerer—she might have ideas about the cub too. I *hoped* she did.

My phone rang as I was cruising down I-5, the autumn rain pattering on the soft-top roof of the Jeep. There wasn't anywhere to pull over, so I answered it on the speaker system and hoped for the best.

"This is Val." I didn't recognize the number, but it was a local area code.

"Valmeyjar Thorvald?" a man asked, surprising me by getting the pronunciation right. My Norwegian mother, who said we were descended from Vikings, had named me after an Old Norse term for the Valkyries. It meant death maiden. She claimed she'd been surprised when I became an assassin, but I wasn't sure I believed her.

"Just Val is fine. Who is this?"

"Lieutenant Reynolds. Colonel Willard gave me your notes to translate."

"Oh?" I hadn't expected to hear from anyone in her office, not after she'd snubbed me all through our meeting.

"The one in ogrish is an address."

"One Cave Misty Loop Lane?" I was curious if Big Mama had been honest with me.

"That's right," he said with surprise.

If I had known he would call me, I wouldn't have needed to spend eighty dollars on meat or tramp through the park this afternoon. At least I'd gotten an extra tip from the male ogre.

"And the other note?"

"I've confirmed that it's written in one of the dragon languages. We have some notes in our linguistics library here with examples of their writing, and one of the symbols matches up."

"One? Does that mean you couldn't translate it?"

"We don't have a dictionary for any of their languages. We've been trying to piece together our own Rosetta Stone from examples we've found in the language books from other species, but... we're not there yet. May I ask where you found the note?"

"In a sack with a glowing silver tiger cub."

Judging by the silence, that also surprised him. "Maybe it's from a species that dragons originally found and named."

"Do dragons keep tigers as pets?"

"I don't know. I was kind of joking."

I wasn't in the mood to be joked with, but I kept from saying something sarcastic. This guy was being a lot more helpful than his colonel.

"We know very little about dragons," he added, "except that they're rulers on many of the other worlds in the portal network. They're often the ones the refugees who flee here say that they were escaping."

"As long as they don't come to Earth, I will go on pretending that they don't exist. Is Willard still going up to Bellingham?"

"She already left. We have an agent missing up there."

I took the James Street exit and headed west. "Did she go alone?"

"She took Captain Rodriguez. Don't worry about the colonel though. She's armed and very capable. She studies martial arts, shoots Hawkeye at the range, and outruns most of the rest of us on any of the unit runs that go over five miles. She's really fit for someone that old."

That old was probably only a few years past forty, but to a twenty-five-year-old lieutenant, that might be ancient. At least he believed Willard could still kick ass and didn't need a walker and soft foods.

"There's someone up there who's scary and dangerous by ogre standards, so tell her to watch out."

"Is that someone at that address?"

"Might be." I decided not to mention that my sources were two sausage-obsessed ogres.

"I'll let her know. I think she's checking our agent's hotel and investigating the murder sites today."

I almost told the lieutenant that I would drive up in the morning, but Willard hadn't wanted my help and might not appreciate an assassin butting into her investigation. I would go on my own. Maybe *entirely* on my own if I could talk Nin into watching the cub. That encounter at the ogre cave could have turned into a disaster if one of them had caught her. I didn't need her stealing chickens from Mr. Scary and Dangerous.

"I have one more thing for you, Ms. Thorvald."

"What?"

"The colonel said to look up Michael Kwon, formerly Sergeant Kwon."

My fingers tightened around the steering wheel. "Did you find something?"

"I had one of our moles—a werewolf who works for us from time to time—go to Rupert's and drop a few bucks here and there. One of the trolls pulled out a rumpled, poorly photocopied wanted poster with his face and name on it. Someone is offering five thousand dollars for his delivery. The poster says he has to be alive."

"*Someone?* Did he get a copy of the poster? Where's he supposed to be delivered?"

"The guy who had it wouldn't give it up, but the werewolf took a photo. The person offering the bounty isn't named. It says to bring Kwon to the castle in Bellingham for payment."

"A castle in Bellingham located at One Cave Misty Loop Lane by chance?" Could a castle be in a cave? Maybe something had been lost in the translation to ogrish.

"There wasn't an address, and we don't know of anything up there that would constitute a castle. Our mole didn't either, but he said he would try to find out. For a price."

"I've got money." Not a lot of it, but if I could afford sausages for ogres, I could afford to pay a werewolf for information.

"Willard said our office would cover the mole and his bribes because Kwon was former army."

"Oh."

I hadn't truly expected Willard to help out, not after she'd made it clear she didn't approve of me or my methods.

"Thanks," I made myself add, though the idea of being indebted to Willard was distasteful. I would swallow that distaste if the army helped me find Michael.

"You're welcome, ma'am." The lieutenant hung up.

A bounty poster that had been distributed among the magical community. Whatever had Michael gotten himself into?

I glanced over at the tiger. "And how are you involved?"

She appeared to be asleep. Had my treasure-hunting best friend stolen the tiger cub from someone? Someone who wanted her cub back?

That didn't make sense now for the same reason it hadn't made sense before. If someone had been on Michael's boat to kidnap him—and the dead ogre outside suggested it had happened right there in the marina—they couldn't have missed the cub. Yes, she had been under the covers, but the ogres would have sensed her the same way I had.

"Unless you hid yourself from them," I mused, "and you didn't hide yourself from me. Because you could tell I would be a friend? Or Michael told you about me, and you were able to understand him?"

I didn't know how much intelligence to ascribe to the cub, but I also wasn't prepared to call it chance that she'd lured Big Mama out of her camp where I could talk to her one on one.

The cub mewed plaintively. Her wrist and tail hung limply over the front of the seat.

"I sure hope you're just tired because you had a big day, and not because you're waning away from lack of nourishment." My throat tightened at the thought of the cub dying because I couldn't figure out what to feed her.

This gave me another reason to find Michael as quickly as possible. Whatever he'd gotten himself into, he ought to know what the cub was and how to take care of her. He had better.

CHAPTER 8

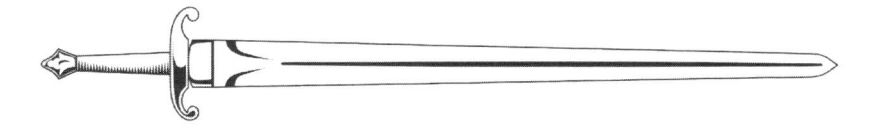

FOG BLANKETED PIONEER SQUARE, CURLING around the totem pole and trees near Nin's food truck and muting the streetlamps. This late, there was parking nearby, and the meters weren't running. Since the cub was sleeping, I left her inside the Jeep.

The Crying Tiger food truck was closed for the night, but I sensed Nin inside and rapped out the secret knock on the door. She was only one-quarter gnome, so her aura was much diminished compared to a full-blooded magical being, but I had no trouble detecting her from so close.

Even though she could probably detect and recognize me, too, she slid open her peephole before opening the door. Every time I visited, her black hair was dyed a different color. Tonight, it was pale green and pulled back into a spunky ponytail wrapped by a forest-green Scrunchie. Her dark eyes were warm as our gazes met—when she stood in the truck and I stood on the bricks of the square, we were the same height.

"Come in, Val," she said in her clear, formal English, her accent barely noticeable. "Do you need ammunition?"

"I do. And some of your special grenades too." I stepped into the cubby in the back of the truck, counters, racks of tools, and boxes of parts and ammo to either side of the narrow aisle. Completed weapons hung on pegboards, everything from wavy kris daggers to purse-sized pistols to automatic rifles, all of them altered from their originals or made from scratch. She'd built my own Fezzik based loosely on the Heckler & Koch MP7.

"You will go into battle?"

"That seems more and more likely with each passing hour, yes." I laid a couple of hundred-dollar bills on the counter and tried not to think about my dwindling reserves.

"Excellent. I always keep ammunition for you in stock. You are one of my most frequent customers."

"Does that mean I get a discount?"

"No." She swept the hundreds into a cash envelope. "But I will throw in extra grenades."

"That seems fair. I've got something in the Jeep that I'd like you to take a look at, too, if you don't mind."

"Certainly. It is dark out there, yes?" She pulled a compact flashlight out of a drawer stuffed to the brim with tools.

"Yeah, but its fur glows."

Nin blinked at me. "You wish me to look at something… furry?"

"It's not a weapon. Except to plucked chickens."

"You are confusing me, Val. I am not a veterinarian. I do not know about animals."

"Come look, anyway." As I turned toward the door, I sensed another magical being outside. A goblin? My first thought was that he must be one of Nin's customers, but he had stopped out in the street. By my Jeep?

Alarm flashed through me, and I flung open the door and ran toward the vehicle. I'd locked the doors, but goblins had the mechanical aptitude and propensity for taking things faster than practiced car strippers.

A short green-skinned figure in a trench coat stood on the running board of my Jeep as he peered through the tinted window on the passenger side.

I drew my gun and asked, "Lose something?" in a hard voice.

Goblins were rarely involved in anything more nefarious than theft, so I didn't plan to shoot him, even if it turned out he'd been trying to break in, but a surge of protectiveness coursed through me. If he had been planning on stealing the cub, I would do my best to scare the little hoodlum.

The goblin spun, slipped off the running board, but recovered and landed on his feet. He flung his hands up. His short white hair stuck up in all directions, and his wide yellow eyes stared up at me. He was only three and a half feet tall.

"The Mythic Murderer," he whispered, one of my other monikers in the magical community.

I didn't know whether to be flattered or not that so many of them recognized me. This goblin wasn't familiar to me.

"That's my Jeep. It doesn't like strangers hanging all over it."

"This is yours?" He reached back and touched the black paint. "Do you know what's inside?"

I almost inventoried my first-aid kit, tire jack, and camping gear for him, but he had to have sensed the cub. "Do you?"

"I believe…" He looked at my gun, but he also climbed back on the running board to peer in the window again.

I strode forward, intending to grab him by the collar of his coat to haul him away, but Nin ran up and gripped my arm.

"Please do not hurt Brugak, Val. He is one of my customers."

"Yes, it is true." Brugak turned back and opened one side of his trench coat to reveal the hilt of a pistol jutting out of his waistband. "I am packing heat. *Nin's* heat." He smiled and winked at her.

"I have told you not to flirt with me, Brugak," Nin said sternly.

"I can't help it. You're part gnome and so cute. You even dyed your hair green for me." He rubbed one of his green cheeks.

"Are you sure you don't want me to hurt him?" I asked Nin.

She hesitated. "He pays well for my goods."

"He has money?"

"He pays in barter that I can use in my business. Steel, gunpowder, halves of cows."

Halves of cows? How did that work?

"Has it ever occurred to you that it's odd that your business can use all those things?" I asked.

"You know I have two businesses."

"I can supply anything you need." Brugak bowed, which caused him to fall off the running board again. He recovered and smiled up at me. Or possibly my chest.

Given his height, I was willing to give him the benefit of the doubt that my chest might be on the way to my eyes from his angle.

"But I am most curious about your passenger." He pointed toward the Jeep door, peered all around, and lowered his voice. "Is that a Del'nothian tiger?"

"It's some kind of tiger. A cub." Normally, I wouldn't give information to a stranger—especially a stranger this strange—but if he knew more than I did and was willing to share... "I was just about to ask Nin if she knew anything about the tiger, since I acquired it somewhat accidentally."

"Accidentally?" Brugak breathed. "How is that possible?" His gaze lifted from my chest to my neck.

My charm-filled thong was under my shirt, but his senses would have told him about the magical trinkets. He squinted, as if he were trying to see through my shirt with X-ray vision.

"You do not have the linked charm, I do not think. How is that possible?"

"You tell me."

He scratched his head. "I cannot. A Del'nothian tiger cannot exist in this realm without one of the control charms. At least I do not believe so."

"What world are these tigers from?" I had heard of most of the worlds over the years and Del'noth didn't ring a bell.

"World? They are from a *realm*."

"Uh." Were we losing something in the translation? The goblin spoke in English, but as I'd learned, there were plenty of words, especially pertaining to magic, that did not have an equivalent in my language.

"The special realm that they and the dragons made long ago."

Dragons? Maybe Lieutenant Reynolds had been right. Maybe that had been the dragon word for this realm.

"How do you get to it? A portal?" As far as I knew, only dragons and very powerful magic users from the various races could create portals between the worlds. Few of the refugees that fled to Earth had that power, so it was a one-way trip for most of them. Meaning there was no way I could send the cub home, unless someone came to get her.

"No. Only the charms allow travel there and only for the tigers themselves."

My head was starting to hurt. "So how could one have left?"

"I don't know. It is possible I am wrong, and that is *not* a Del'nothian tiger, but I have seen one before. I was almost *eaten* by one before."

"Are you joking?"

"I suppose, but only because they do not eat on our worlds. One was sent to hunt me down. That is why I fled to Earth. Never did I think to see one of those tigers here."

I barely heard anything after the word eat. *They do not eat on our worlds.* This *did* sound like my new furry friend.

"May I see it?" Brugak turned his bright eyes on me.

"No," I said, more out of reflex than logic. I doubted he would try to steal the cub with me standing two feet away.

"May I?" Nin asked.

"Yeah."

"Goodness, Mythic Murderer," Brugak said. "I would not be so foolish as to cross you. I know you have slain many of my kind."

"I don't think I've ever slain a goblin. I only kill murderers and really bad guys. You appear mediocrely bad at worst."

He spread his hand over his chest. "I am not bad at all."

"No? Where do you get the halves of cows you bring to Nin?"

"From the cow repository."

"Also known as a farmer's field?"

"I do not know who owns the fields. But cows are large and can feed an entire clan of goblins for a moon."

"Yeah, I hear they feed farmers for many moons too."

A troubled expression crossed Nin's face. Maybe it hadn't occurred to her that Brugak's cows were stolen.

"The cub is what I wanted to show you, Nin." I holstered Fezzik, certain I could catch the goblin if he did try anything.

Nin smiled and patted the pistol on my thigh. "I must admit that it surprises me that you choose my firearm to draw first when your sword is so much more powerful, but it also pleases me."

"I've found it's good to please the woman who makes your magical ammo." I didn't admit that the gun was my go-to weapon because I'd been handling firearms for a lot longer than blades. It hadn't been until

I'd defeated the zombie and claimed Chopper as my own that I'd started to train with the sword. Years later, and more hours of practice than I could count, I was handy enough with the weapon, but the gun felt more natural in my grip.

Besides, I was fond of taking care of enemies from a distance whenever possible. My organs were more likely to stay on the inside if I didn't get close enough to shifters or other fanged or taloned creatures for evisceration.

When I opened the door, the cub was still sleeping and barely lifted her head. My uneasy certainty that more than fatigue affected her returned to me.

In the dim lighting, her fur glowed faint silver.

"It *is* a Del'Nothian tiger," Brugak breathed and stroked his hand over her side.

The cub's tail flicked slightly, but that was the only sign of objection—or acknowledgment.

"Is she sick?" Nin asked.

"I don't know. She was fine earlier. She helped me find some ogres. Energetically."

"Del'Nothian tigers are absolutely energetic." Brugak rubbed his butt at some memory, perhaps of having a chomp taken out of it. "But they can only stay for a certain amount of time away from their realm before they must return to feed and rejuvenate. How long has this one been here?"

"I'm not sure when she got here, but I've had her for almost twenty-four hours." It seemed like it had been much longer. The thought elicited a yawn, and I grimaced at the idea of going up to Bellingham tonight, but if Willard was already up there and the cub was in danger, I doubted I would be able to sleep tonight anyway. Besides, just because Michael's bounty poster had said he was to be captured alive didn't mean whoever had paid for it planned to *keep* him alive.

"Interesting," Brugak said. "I didn't think they could stay away from their realm for that long."

"What happens if they do?"

"I thought they were automatically yanked back when they needed rest, but I also thought they were all linked to charms and that the power to summon and release them came from them."

"I didn't see a charm." I frowned as I thought back to Michael's ransacked boat. Was it possible someone had taken the charm and not the cub? But if so, why? Why not take both if they were linked?

"What happens if she does *not* automatically go back to her home?" Nin had crept forward and was taking her turn petting the tiger.

Brugak shrugged. "I don't know, but she may die."

My insides clenched, and I shook my head. "That's *not* going to happen."

"You will go into battle tonight?" Nin asked me.

"Damn right, I will."

"I will get your ammo and grenades."

CHAPTER 9

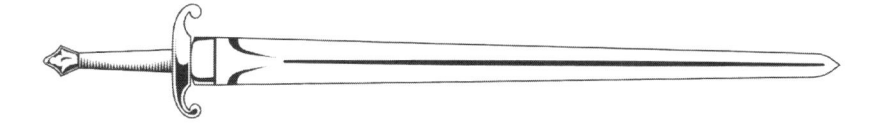

NIN WAS KIND ENOUGH TO give me several of her beef-and-rice meals along with the ammo and grenades, so I left for Bellingham straight from her truck. It was after ten, and I was fighting yawns after being up so late the previous night, but I drove north out of the city with determination.

I left the fog in Seattle behind but traded it for rain that picked up as I drove through Everett. It hammered the windshield and formed puddles on the freeway that ducks could have paddled in.

The phone rang before I got through Marysville. Julie.

I didn't want to answer it and almost didn't, but it was possible Michael's kidnapper had called his family and she had information.

"Val here." I answered over the Jeep's speaker system, not wanting to take my focus from the road with the rain making visibility poor. At least there wasn't much traffic.

"Have you learned anything about Michael yet?"

That meant she hadn't heard anything. I regretted answering.

"I have a couple of leads I'm investigating."

"That means no, right?" She sounded frustrated and cranky.

Probably tired and worried, I told myself, trying to see things from her side. Julie and I had never gotten along because she thought I was the bad influence who'd lured Michael away from his solid finance job, but that wasn't true. His family had pressured him into that career, and he'd hated it. If it hadn't been treasure hunting, it would have been something else. Something they didn't approve of.

"I got the address that was in the dead ogre's pocket translated," I said. "I'm heading to Bellingham to check it out."

Google Maps had laughed at me when I'd tried to click for a street view of Misty Loop Lane. None of their camera cars had ever ambled down it to take photos. The best I'd been able to tell from the satellite view was that it was a dirt road. I hadn't spotted any caves or castles along it and hoped I wasn't going on a wild goose chase.

"Bellingham? Who kidnaps someone and takes them to Bellingham?"

"I don't know, Julie. I'll call you when I find him."

"Is there anything I can do to help?"

I wanted to end the conversation so I could focus on driving—if anything, the rain was getting worse—but I didn't want to snap at her. "Not unless you can get his phone unlocked and it holds all his secrets."

"The phone carrier said the only way to unlock it is to reset it."

At which point, his secrets would be gone. If they were on there at all. I had a feeling his biggest secret was sleeping on my passenger seat.

The cub was so quiet that I reached over to touch her and make sure she was still breathing. It seemed impossible that such a young vibrant being could be in danger of dying, but if she truly didn't belong in this world and weakened the longer she was in it...

My throat tightened up with emotion. I'd barely known the cub for a full night and day, but I didn't want to see her die.

She barely stirred at my touch, but she was still breathing. That was something.

"I'll let you know if I learn anything new," I said.

"Good. You better... I hope he doesn't..." Julie's own throat sounded tight with emotion.

I was worried about Michael, too, but I was good at my job, and I believed I could find him, so I hadn't yet started to think of the possibility that I wouldn't. Or that I would be too late.

"He wouldn't know about any of this stuff if it weren't for you," Julie said, the accusation hanging in the air.

"I know."

I'd never tried to deny that. One of the reasons we'd broken up was the same reason I'd broken up with my ex-husband. The bad guys that I hunted down and killed tended to have brothers or sisters—or pack- or clan-mates—who came after me and tried to avenge their deaths. More than one innocent bystander had been taken out by drive-by shooters that had been aiming at me. That was horrifying enough, and a guilt I lived with every day, but the idea of losing someone I cared deeply for that way…

Julie hung up.

The rain pounding on the Jeep's soft top sounded like hail. Or bullets. My headlights barely pierced the water gushing from the sky, and I started to envision cows out on the interstate and how I'd never see them in time to swerve or stop. Wind railed at the doors, and I finally gave up and pulled over to the side of the highway to wait for the rain to abate. I wouldn't do Michael any good if I ran off the road and died in a crash in some farmer's field. Or in their cow repository. I snorted at the goblin's words, but at least he'd given me intelligence on the cub.

As the rain kept hammering down, I leaned my head back on the rest and closed my eyes, thinking I should have waited until morning to leave.

But Willard was already up there, possibly getting herself in trouble, and Michael was…

"Where are you, Michael?" I murmured.

A stack of bills sat on the table in front of me, payment for the completion of my last assignment. My focus was on the golden liquid in the mug in front of me. It had started out in a shot glass, but that had been insufficient for my needs.

My front door opened, and I had Fezzik out and pointing at it before the intruder walked in. It was Michael.

I lowered the weapon to the table. "Some people knock before they barge into people's houses."

"This is a studio apartment with a view of a brick wall, not a house, and I figured you'd welcome my entrance, given the triumphant success of our last rendezvous." He wriggled his eyebrows, unconcerned that he could have ended up with a bullet in his chest. Or maybe he trusted that my reflexes were better than that.

"The last time we rendezvoused, we had sex in the Jeep."

"Triumphantly."

I grunted, far less ebullient over it. The gear shift had made me second-guess our choice that night numerous times.

Michael closed the door and ambled over to sit opposite me at the table, resting a thick book next to Fezzik's muzzle. "Nice wad of cash."

"I got paid for the Bellevue Bandit."

"The Bellevue Bandit who kept murdering the people in the meat-packing plants he was robbing?"

"He won't be murdering anyone else."

"That's good. Was he a shifter?"

"A troll with some magic to mask himself. If Hobbs hadn't brought in someone who could see through that—" I tapped my chest, *"—the troll might have gone on evading the law."*

"So, you were key to stopping crime. Again." Michael grinned. *"Why do you look so glum? And what are you drinking? That looks more concentrated than your usual poison."* He waved to a six-pack of hard cider resting on the counter by the fridge.

"Applejack."

"Very colonial. I'm sure George Washington would have approved."

"If you mock my drink, there will be no sex tonight."

"I thought that was already off the table, given that you greeted me with a gun and a glower."

"Isn't that how I usually greet you?"

"I suppose it is. Yet I'm here anyway." He flashed another grin. *"You're lucky to have me."*

"Yeah." I sipped from the mug and set it back down. *"The troll bandit had a kid. A whole community of trolls that he was providing for. I tracked him back to them, confronted him, and killed him. He was still wearing the shirt with his last victim's blood on it, so there was no questioning his guilt, but... I wish his family hadn't been watching."*

"Maybe if he had a family, he shouldn't have been murdering the people he stole from."

"He was a berserker troll—temper more explosive than fire ants crawling up your leg. I'm not sure he meant to kill people, but when he

got backed into a corner…" I shrugged, wrestling with my feelings over the day. "Hobbs wanted his head. I brought in his head. He wouldn't have been backed into corners if he hadn't been thieving."

"So that should be a celebratory drink rather than a drowning-your-sorrows drink." Michael arched his eyebrows. "Right?"

"Yeah. I just keep seeing the kid. And wondering if he'll try to come hunt me down someday."

"How old was he?"

Another shrug. "Six or seven maybe. It's hard to tell with trolls."

"You've got at least six years before he'll be able to threaten you with more than a slingshot."

"Maybe."

Michael scrutinized me, maybe guessing that this wasn't the only thing contributing to my glum mood. Every time I made a new enemy, I worried that it would be as likely to come back to haunt him as me. Was I being selfish by allowing myself the comfort and camaraderie of a relationship?

"How's Thad? And Amber?" Michael was the only person who knew about my business and the magical community and who also knew about my previous life. Or maybe it was more appropriate to call it my interim life.

I'd met and married Thad in the army, and we'd had Amber after getting out, at which point I'd vowed to settle down and lead a normal life, not be anyone's hired killer. I'd gotten as far as taking business classes from U-Dub, envisioning some future where I balanced books and helped Thad with his software company. Then an influx of magical refugees had come to Seattle, murders had skyrocketed, the police had been flummoxed by their mystical powers, and I'd made the choice to return to this work. As a freelancer this time—not some obedient soldier—able to call my own shots and continue to be a mom and a wife. Or so I'd thought.

Until the night a pack of werewolves, angry that I'd taken out one of their buddies, tracked me down at my house. They hadn't cared that he'd been a criminal. They'd come for me anyway. Out in the street in front of our suburban house, I'd fought off six werewolves and nearly died.

Thad and Amber had slept through it all. I was glad they had, glad that I'd been awake and sensed the shifters approaching before they'd lobbed the grenades they'd carried through the bedroom windows.

The next week, I'd left. It had been hard to walk away, to file divorce papers, but I'd realized that I couldn't have a normal life and a family and also be an assassin. I'd had to choose. Years later, I wasn't positive I'd made the right choice, but I did know that a lot of people were alive today who would have otherwise been dead if I hadn't stayed in the business. This was what I'd been trained to do, what I had the blood to do. And because I'd left and done my best to make my relationship with Thad and Amber disappear to the public, they were still alive too.

"Val?" Michael nudged me with his foot under the table, his humor replaced by a frown. "Are they okay?"

"Yeah. Sorry. As far as I know, they are. I've cut all ties to them so nobody can trace them to me. As far as my enemies go, I'm just a single gal with no ties to anyone. Except you."

"They know about me?" He rested a hand on his chest. "I'm touched."

"You had better not be. Maybe you should wear a pizza-delivery uniform when you come to my apartment."

"A lot of pornos start that way."

"You're an aficionado, are you?"

"Well, I'm male." He slid the book onto the table and opened it. "And I'm here to take your mind off your worries."

"With a book? Are you going to read me bedtime stories?"

"I could. I've been researching magical blades. This book has a whole bunch of famous ones crafted by dwarves thousands of years ago and then lost over the ages. It's believed that some of them were stolen by refugees fleeing the Cosmic Realms to the wild worlds. Such as Earth."

"Are you trying to find one for yourself?"

"I have been admiring yours." He gazed at the sword harness draped across an adjacent chair, Chopper sheathed in the scabbard. "It's quite remarkable. You could probably sell it and fully fund your retirement."

"I'd have to go back to the boom-boom method of killing magical bad guys in the interim." I couldn't imagine retiring, not while I was still qualified to do this work, not while so few others were.

"Boom-boom? Did they teach you that in the army?"

"Absolutely they did. That's where you throw as many grenades as you can at vampires, zombies, shifters, and the like, and hope that the power of physics overrides the power of magic."

"Does it?"

"Often, but it has a tendency to take down nearby buildings, bridges, and small mountains."

"Inconvenient." Michael flipped to a bookmarked page in the thick tome. "I was perusing this earlier and thought this one looks a bit like yours. What do you think?"

Curious, I looked. But the black ink sketch wasn't detailed. "I doubt Chopper has ever been written up in a book. I got it from a zombie, not a dwarf."

"Maybe the zombie got it from a dwarf."

"The blade is still sharp. I'm sure it's not thousands of years old."

"Maybe not." He flipped to another bookmark. "This is one I'm researching. It was reputed to be stolen by gnomish pirates centuries ago and brought to a lush and damp wild world full of forests and buried in a cache by a quiet inlet of the sea. Sounds a bit like Puget Sound, doesn't it?"

"Sounds like a ton of places on Earth. And probably even more places in all of the realms."

"Maybe." He shrugged easily, closed the book, and stood.

"Are you leaving?" A tendril of panic curled around my soul as the memory of the troll boy's eyes flashed through my mind along with the certainty that I didn't want to be alone.

"Do you want me to?" He stopped beside my chair and rested his hand on the back of my head.

I leaned my forehead against his stomach. I didn't want to need anyone, but... sometimes I did. "No."

"Good. I was just going to get my pizza-delivery uniform."

"You're hilarious."

"Someone has to balance out your gloominess, Eeyore."

A horn blasted on the freeway, jerking me out of the slumber I hadn't intended to find. A semitruck roared past, wheels spraying water.

The dream faded from my mind but not the memory of it, because that conversation had actually happened. It had been more than a year ago, when we'd still been romantically involved, but I wondered if my mind was trying to tell me something in dredging it up.

Michael had finished his quest for that sword without finding it—though he'd discovered a cache with a few magical trinkets in it, one of which he'd traded to me for a foot massage—and it was hard to imagine it tying in with a baby tiger and maulings in Bellingham, but I would keep my ears open for anything about swords.

But first, I had Misty Loop Lane to visit. It was still raining but not as hard as before, and visibility had improved, so I pulled back onto the highway and continued north.

CHAPTER 10

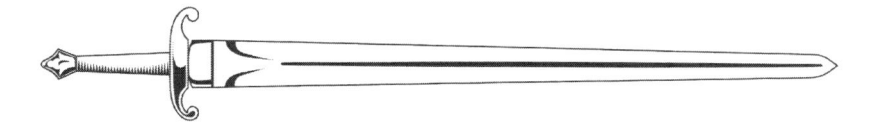

IT WAS THREE A.M. BY the time I reached Bellingham, drove off into the boonies, and found the entrance to the dirt road half hidden by trees and dense undergrowth. There wasn't a street sign, but the GPS insisted this was the place.

It had led me astray before, so I didn't trust it very far. I was already on a gravel road in the middle of nowhere. I hadn't seen another car for twenty minutes, and it had been miles since I'd passed the last driveway. I'd passed a few old logging roads marked by numbers but little more. The satellite map showed nothing but trees where I was, and I was skeptical that I would find an address up this dirt road.

Despite the remoteness, the headlights played over fresh tracks in the mud of the turnoff, and a broken branch dangled at the edge of the windshield. Someone had been this way recently. Willard? Ogres in a van driving the kidnapped Michael? Both?

Glad for the Jeep, I headed up the lumpy, muddy road, turning on the high-beams in the hope that I wouldn't miss One Cave Misty Loop Lane. I had a feeling there wasn't going to be an address marker or even a mailbox, but maybe the fresh tracks would remain followable and would lead me to the right spot.

"Here's hoping."

According to the map, the road meandered and curved through hilly terrain for a few miles before coming out on a forest-service road that eventually led back into town. At least, if I found nothing, I wouldn't have to turn around and come back the same way.

The Jeep bumped and tilted as I did my best to avoid the potholes. A plaintive "merow" came from the passenger seat.

"Sorry," I told my groggy cub. "I'm afraid the road-maintenance standards out here are low."

The cub stretched a paw over and rested it on my thigh. She gazed up at me with those green eyes, eyes that seemed to be asking for a kind of help that I didn't know how to give. I rested a hand on her head and rubbed a soft ear.

"Let me know if you sense anything," I told her. "I'm sure your range extends farther than mine."

She shifted her paw from my thigh to the keys dangling out of the ignition and batted at the *Princess Bride* keychain that read, *Have fun storming the castle!*

"Careful with that. That's a priceless artifact from my childhood."

"Merow?"

"It's from one of the first movies I ever saw. Mom had to raise me alone and never had much money, so she fixed up an old school bus into a home. We spent a lot of time camping out on state land until I was ten and one of her friends let us park the bus in their back yard. Then I got to play inside with her girls and experience television and the VCR—like a normal kid. Mom never got into movies, but I watched *The Princess Bride* about five hundred times. I even named my gun after Fezzik from the movie." I tapped the holster, though the cub was far more interested in the keychain than my story. "The sword was named after the junkyard dog in *Stand By Me*. Chopper, sic balls. That's what counts as a memorable line when you're ten."

As I drove and rambled, more trying to keep myself awake and entertain the cub than out of any expectation of interaction, I scanned the moss-draped branches and dense undergrowth encroaching from either side of the dirt road. A few more years, and the road would likely disappear altogether.

Between the rain and the dark, my headlights seemed insufficient for a search. Since I had a charm that allowed me to see in the dark, I turned them off and activated it, hoping that more would become apparent. But the dense forest was much the same. I could just see it better.

The lack of side roads surprised me, especially if this had originally been a logging area. Signs or an indication that anything was back here were equally lacking.

"I have a feeling it might take magic to find this address."

Even though I could sense magical artifacts and beings, that might not be enough. That thought grew stronger and stronger as I continued without seeing anything. The fresh tire marks in the mud also continued, but I decided that whoever had come before me had likely driven all the way through without finding anything.

That was when light grew noticeable, coming from around a bend ahead. Since any type of illumination flared intensely bright when the charm was working, I deactivated it, but I didn't turn on my headlights.

I sensed something magical in the same direction as that light. Not a person but a tool or weapon, perhaps. It felt similar to Fezzik.

Unfortunately, I didn't sense ogres or any other magical beings that might have hinted I was on the right track.

The headlights of an SUV came into view, and I winced at their brightness, then did my best to pull off to the side so it could pass. Instead, the SUV stopped, and the door opened. The driver left the headlights on, the vehicle positioned so they blinded me if I looked at it. That meant I couldn't identify who was coming, beyond the outline of a long coat and a rain hat.

Though I suspected it was Willard—who else would be out here?—I unholstered Fezzik and rested my finger on the trigger.

"That look like Willard to you?" I asked my seatmate as I rolled down the window.

"Merow?"

"You met her. Though she halfway accused you of mauling people up here, so maybe it wasn't the best introduction."

"That you skulking in the dark, Thorvald?" Willard's southern drawl came from under the hat. Her hand was also resting on a firearm, though it wasn't the source of the magic I'd sensed.

"I'm driving, not skulking."

"With your lights off?"

"I have a charm that lets me see in the dark. Unless someone's headlights are blinding me."

"Handy."

"Not at the current moment, no. You find anything out here?"

Willard stopped by the side mirror and studied me, but with the lights at her back, I couldn't read her expression. "I'm guessing from your question that you haven't," she said.

"Not yet."

"Nothing magical out here that any of your charms can sense?"

"Just whatever's in your car."

She hesitated, either because she didn't want to tell me what it was, or she wasn't sure what it was.

"Captain Rodriguez has magical bullets for his magical gun," she eventually said.

"Is it aimed at me?"

"In your general direction."

"Comforting."

"I figured it was you, since Reynolds said he gave you the address." Willard didn't sound like she approved or wanted me here. Tough.

"I got a translation on my own from the ogres at Shoreview Park, so I was coming one way or another."

Willard looked back at her SUV and made a patting motion, hopefully telling her officer that he didn't need to hold his gun on me. "We went through here once and were going to make another pass in case we missed something, then head into town and study the USGS maps we got by better light. The GPS directed us here, so we thought this would be it, but…"

"Mine thinks this is Misty Loop Lane too."

Her phone rang, and she moved away from me to answer it.

"Who's calling you at 3:30 in the morning?" I asked.

"Colonel Willard," she answered, ignoring me.

I caught a few words from the caller—a medical examiner saying she'd finished an autopsy. For Willard's missing agent? Or was this someone who'd been killed by the feline claws? Whoever the subject of the procedure had been, his heart had stopped.

"That shouldn't be possible," Willard said. "He was barely thirty and fit."

"…might have been electrocuted."

"Electrocuted?" Willard scowled down at the ground. "When he was found next to someone whose throat was torn out by a tiger?"

"Tiger?" I mouthed, glancing at the cub. She'd stopped playing with the keychain and was sniffing at the damp air wafting in through my open window.

I missed whatever the medical examiner said, but Willard's next words were, "I know, I know, it's bigger than a tiger. Whatever it is, we'll find it."

"We also found something on your man. I don't know if it's more than a souvenir knickknack, but you'll probably want to see it."

"I'll be there in an hour," Willard said.

"Bring coffee."

"Always." She hung up and returned to my window. "Why don't you keep hunting around here, and let me know if you find anything?"

"I want to go see the body and whatever the medical examiner found." I would be willing to come back here once it got light and I had a better shot at seeing evidence of people—or ogres—leaving the road, but the mystery with the body and some unnamed item sounded like a better lead.

"You're not on the case."

"And yet here I am."

"Annoyingly, yes."

"You could use my help."

"I told you before," Willard said. "I looked at your record. You're a reckless maverick who doesn't think the rules apply to her. Even when you were in the army, you frequently failed to obey your superiors and ended up with more disciplinary actions than a drunken sailor on his first shore leave in a year."

"Only because my superiors didn't understand me and nurture my creative streak."

"I'm sure I would side with your superiors."

"I'm sure you would, too, but look, if some magic was used to kill your agent, I might be able to detect it."

"Your record failed to mention that you're an eavesdropper."

"You have to read further. It's in the appendix."

Willard shook her head and stepped back. "You're not coming, Thorvald. I can't stop you from looking for your friend, but you're not on my team."

"Fine, but I'm going to look next for my friend at the morgue."

"We don't need your help."

"*He* does."

She glowered over her shoulder at me as she stalked back to her SUV. "You'll find that the front door is locked to random civilians."

"I have a lock-picking charm too," I called after her.

"Merow?" the cub inquired.

"It's true," I told her, though I doubted that was truly a comment on the conversation. "I've been collecting this stuff for years." I waved at charms on my leather thong, then put the Jeep back into gear.

Feeling a touch peevish, I drove past Willard as she was getting in, gave her a cheerful wave, and plugged in the address for the Whatcom County Medical Examiner, determined to beat them there. I hadn't mentioned my stealth charm to Willard. Even if she called ahead and tried to warn someone that I was coming, it wouldn't keep me out.

In the rear-view mirror, the SUV turned around quickly but awkwardly on the narrow road, then came after me. But my Jeep had more clearance and better tires for off-roading, and I smirked as I outpaced them.

"Time to find out how stopped hearts, giant tigers, and murders are tied in with Michael's disappearance," I murmured.

CHAPTER 11

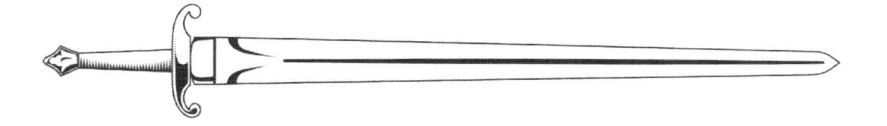

AS I'D PROMISED WILLARD, I had little trouble sneaking into the building without being seen. The back door was unlocked, and there weren't any security or police officers waiting to apprehend me. Since the rain had picked up again, I was glad there weren't any obstacles to bypass, though I had expected Willard to warn someone that an interloper might show up. Maybe she hadn't wanted to risk putting anybody in my *maverick* path. Or maybe she secretly believed that I *could* help.

Even though I'd had assignments in this county before, I hadn't been in the health center before, and it took me a while to hunt down the stairway to the basement that led down to the morgue. Sensing a magical item somewhere on that level made me pause. I didn't think it was a weapon. Could it be the *knickknack* the medical examiner had mentioned to Willard?

I found the morgue and was about to enter, checking to ensure my camouflaging charm was still activated, when voices sounded in the hallway behind me.

Willard and Rodriguez had arrived. Before they came into sight, I slipped into the morgue. I paused to peek out the window in the door as they arrived. Captain Rodriguez was a bullet-shaped man with a bald head and granite jaw. He looked more like an infantry sergeant than an intelligence officer.

I moved away from the door so they wouldn't be close enough to see through my charm's magic when they stepped inside. It crossed my mind to make my presence known, but they might try to kick me out. I also might learn more if nobody knew I was there. Willard had shared more information than I'd expected so far, but she'd also made it clear she didn't want me here.

Two bodies were laid out on exam tables, still zipped into bags. Or maybe already examined and *re*-zipped into bags. The medical examiner was sitting at a desk, her head in her hand, and her eyes closed. Her scrubs and lab coat were rumpled, as if she'd grabbed them out of a dirty-laundry basket in the middle of the night. Maybe she had. She must have been ordered in late—or early—as a favor to Willard.

The magical item I'd been sensing seemed to be located in a folder under her elbow. That would be difficult to extract without her noticing.

She stirred when the officers walked in carrying coffee cups—I wondered where they had found someplace open this early. Bellingham wasn't a big city with copious all-night coffee options.

"Here are the reports for both of them, Colonel." The medical examiner brought two folders to her, including the one with the magical item, then unzipped one of the body bags. "You can take a look at your agent, if you want, but there weren't any physical marks on him, not even burns. And you've already seen the guy who was mauled." She waved to the body closest to them and farthest from me. "The deep lacerations on his throat are indeed what killed him and are in line with what you'd expect from the claws of a very large cougar." She opted for the only large cat indigenous to the area, but I doubted anything indigenous had been killing people. "He also has a broken tibia," she continued, "which likely happened during a fall at the time of the attack."

Captain Rodriguez gave the coffee in his hand to the medical examiner, surprising a thanks from her. The scents from the hot beverages teased the room, and I was almost tired enough to find them appealing, though my interest was in the caffeine, not the coffee, which I detested.

Willard was looking over the reports, so I took the opportunity to step closer to the body that had been electrocuted. That of her agent.

My gut clenched. I recognized him.

That wasn't surprising, since Willard had said he was one of the soldiers in her unit, and I'd occasionally worked with them when Hobbs had been in charge, but I hadn't expected it to be one of the ones I'd liked. Or at least liked to trade snarky comments with. Sergeant O'Sullivan. He'd always tried to get me to sell my sword to him and lamented that it was so much bigger than his.

I struggled for detachment as I surveyed him for evidence of magical tampering—or, more likely, a magical attack. Magic didn't leave a telltale signature, unfortunately, but it could account for sudden deaths without physical signs. Wizards could hurl lightning attacks that would appear to a medical examiner exactly like a lightning strike or other electrocution. Elves and some of the more powerful magical beings could channel telekinetic power from within and use it to squeeze a heart until it stopped beating.

"Davie Thornberg is the name of the civilian?" Willard was reading the second report. "I wish O'Sullivan had checked in and let us know what he was doing. Was this guy a random civilian who happened to be in the hotel with him at the same time as he was attacked, or did O'Sullivan call him in for questioning?" She glanced at the captain. "You looked him up, right?"

"He's a local," Rodriguez said. "A boat mechanic who works at the marina."

"A strange place for tigers to hang out."

The medical examiner raised her eyebrows. "We don't have tigers. We do have cougars."

"Tigers have been on my mind."

I wondered if Michael might have been brought up here by boat rather than in a van. That wouldn't change anything about where he was now, but the ogres might have tramped past this Davie and that was how he'd ended up involved. A witness who'd reported them to O'Sullivan?

"So, are we looking at a cat-shifter wizard, or what?" Willard looked at Rodriguez.

The medical examiner lifted her eyebrows again but didn't appear shocked by the question. She must have seen the occasional body mauled by magic.

"Or a cat shifter *and* a wizard?" Rodriguez suggested.

Or maybe not a shifter at all. I thought of the cub sleeping in my Jeep and wondered if there was a grown-up version of her around. Would the cub react to the body—and whatever scent the predator might have left on it—if I brought her in?

Willard tilted the folder, and the magical item I'd sensed slid out onto her palm. A slender metal stick with an emblem on a hook at the top, it looked like a fancy bookmark.

I concentrated on the magic emanating from it and tried to guess which species had crafted it. The elegance of the work, from what I could see across the room, reminded me of elves, and the magic lingering about it did too.

Just what we needed. Another species involved in the mystery here.

"Nice toothpick," Rodriguez grunted.

"I was thinking bookmark," Willard said.

"That's because you're erudite and stuff."

Willard was erudite? I supposed she wouldn't have been picked to head an intelligence-gathering unit if she was a thug, but she reminded me so much of that drill sergeant I'd had—and she had *definitely* been a thug.

"I'm more into eating than reading," Rodriguez added.

"Are you supposed to admit things like that to a woman?"

"I'm an open book, ma'am."

"A book with pictures?"

"Yup." He grinned.

"You said our agent was the one with it?" Willard asked the medical examiner.

"Yes. He stored it in an interesting place."

Willard dropped it in the folder and wiped her hand on her pants.

"Not *that* interesting." The medical examiner shook her head. "But he had stuffed it in his underwear. His pockets were empty except for his car keys."

"Maybe he thought he would be searched." Rodriguez picked it up and looked it over, then shrugged. "I don't know if it's magical or some useless souvenir or what. Maybe you should call Thorvald in here."

I'd been about to leave to retrieve the cub and walk back in without my stealth charm engaged, but I paused in the doorway, curious if Willard would admit that she could use me.

"Having someone who doesn't follow orders on a team is a good way to get everyone killed," Willard said.

"She can sense magic though. Colonel Hobbs used to call her in to hunt down people we couldn't."

"I don't want a maverick working with our unit. It's a liability. Especially a maverick who skulks in the shadows and doesn't admit she's here spying on us."

I arched my eyebrows. Did she truly know? Or was she guessing? I'd parked in the shadow of a dumpster in an alley behind the building, so she shouldn't have seen my Jeep.

"You think she's here?" Rodriguez looked toward the corners—toward the shadows.

"Yes." Willard didn't look around, but she addressed me directly. "You left wet footprints in the hallway, Thorvald."

Hm, maybe she *was* smarter than I'd thought. Or at least more observant. Colonel Willard Holmes.

I thought about confessing, but I didn't want her to feel smug, so I slipped out and retrieved the cub from the Jeep before returning, this time with my camouflaging charm deactivated.

Willard squinted at me when I walked in, and I had a feeling she was still positive she'd been right.

"You can't bring a pet in here," the medical examiner objected.

I was carrying the cub in my arms—she still hadn't recovered her energy from the day before—and doubted the medical examiner could tell what she was.

"She's not a pet. She's a young tiger from Del'noth." I thought that was what the goblin had said. "A magical tiger."

All three of them looked at the claw-mauled body.

"She's been with me so obviously isn't responsible for that, but I thought she might sense something." As I walked over, the cub did perk her head up. She sniffed the air and tried to climb out of my arms to get to the body.

I set her down, but that didn't help her since she was too short to reach the body. With a little more growing, she would be able to jump that high but not yet. She gave me a flat look with her green eyes, as if to inform me of that fact.

"I can't put you on the table, kid. There's a dead guy on it."

Rodriguez arched his eyebrows. "Does she speak back?"

"Merow." The cub pawed at the base of the table.

"Obviously," I told him. "Unfortunately, my translation charm doesn't have any suggestions as to what she's saying."

The cub walked around the table, sniffing at the air—sniffing toward the body. The body that had been electrocuted didn't hold any interest for her at all.

"Which is too bad," I added, "because I'd like to know if she's aware of any other larger tigers in the area."

Willard squinted at me. "I'd been thinking we're dealing with a feline shifter of some kind."

"It's possible, but this girl was in Michael's boat when I got there. The same night he was kidnapped. By ogres, one of whom died on his dock with that address in his pocket."

"*That address*." Willard snorted. "If that's a real address, I'm not convinced we were on the right road."

"Have you had a chance to look at the USGS maps yet?"

"No." She covered her mouth as she cracked a yawn. "We were talking about doing it next over some food."

"You got any idea what this is, Thorvald?" Rodriguez brought the bookmark tool over to me.

I paused in the middle of reaching for it. Before, I hadn't been able to see the emblem on the top. Now, I could.

"Don't worry," Willard said. "Our good medical examiner promises it wasn't stored inside any body cavities."

"I'm not sure being nestled against somebody's balls is better." But that wasn't why I'd paused, and I finished reaching for it.

"I knew you were in here," Willard growled.

"Yeah. I wanted to hear evidence that you're erudite."

I turned the item over in my hand, then held the emblem toward the light.

"I'll recite some encyclopedias for you later."

"That'll be sure to keep me awake. So… this is a castle." I held it up.

"Brilliant observation," Willard said.

"Didn't Lieutenant Reynolds mention the castle to you?"

Willard looked at Rodriguez, who shook his head. They must not have asked to be apprised of new information related to Michael. After all, they'd come up because of the maulings and their missing agent. It was also possible Reynolds had dug up the tidbit about the bounty after sharing the address with Willard.

"He told me about a bounty out for Michael, some unnamed person offering a reward for him if he was brought alive to the castle in Bellingham."

"There aren't any castles in Bellingham," the medical examiner said.

"There must be." I held up the emblem. "And I have a hunch this is the key."

"The key to the front door or the key that would let us find it from a neglected logging road?" Willard asked.

"I don't know that, but this key is magical."

The cub made a pitiful noise and flopped onto her side on the tile floor. She was under the table, still looking up at the body, but she seemed to have given up on reaching it.

"Your cat doesn't look right," Willard said. "She was a lot perkier this morning when she was swatting at your braid."

"I know." I hesitated, not sure if I should admit my fears, but maybe one of them would know something about this strange species that didn't eat or drink, at least not on Earth. I relayed what the goblin had told me.

"If that's true, being stuck here could kill her." Willard frowned, then knelt beside the cub and stroked her fur. It seemed the hardened army officer had a soft spot for animals.

"That's what I'm afraid of. We need to hurry."

Hurry and do what, I didn't know. All I had were hopes and hunches at this point that everything was tied together and that I'd find a solution for the cub at the same time I found Michael.

"Let's go over those maps first," Willard said. "We're not driving back out to that road so we can stick that bookmark out the window and wave it hopefully at the trees. Not without making sure that truly is Misty Loop Lane."

Though urgency battered at my nerves, I couldn't object to the logic. It had taken nearly an hour to navigate that pothole-filled road the first time, and even if this magical key was linked to the castle, I had no idea if it would help us locate it. I hoped the cub could hold out for a few more hours.

CHAPTER 12

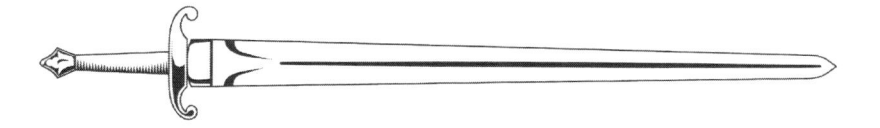

IT WAS STILL EARLY ENOUGH, and dark and rainy enough outside, that we had an entire section at Denny's to ourselves. That was good because Willard spread out maps across three tables. That flummoxed the waitress, who didn't know where to set down our food. I took my sizzling skillet and plopped it down on Puget Sound, not caring if gravy tumbled off onto the map.

Willard glared at me. "These are borrowed. Put that somewhere else."

I considered being recalcitrant, but for all I knew, USGS maps were worth thousands of dollars. I pulled over another table and rested my plate on it, taking bites in between looking at the fields and forests and mountains around Bellingham.

"Here's our road." Willard pointed. "And it doesn't have a label beyond a forest-service number. What makes the GPS map think it's Misty Loop Lane?"

"Do you see anything else called Misty Loop Lane?" Rodriguez asked, his mouth stuffed full of hamburger.

Willard eyed his vigorous chomping. She'd sent her salad back because the lettuce had been limp and brown around the edges, and another one had not appeared. Maybe she was regretting being picky. It had been the only salad on the menu; judging by the grease coating the potatoes in my skillet meal, they didn't cater to the health conscious here.

I took my phone out and ran an internet search for Misty Loop Lane in Bellingham to see if any other addresses came up. I'd already Googled the One Cave address and failed to get any hits, but I hadn't tried the street by itself.

"No mention of it anywhere on the web," I said. "Funny that my map app came up with a hit. Closest match on the web is a Misty Ridge Court."

"Does it look like the kind of place with a castle full of ogre kidnappers?" Willard asked.

"It's a cul-de-sac with three houses and is across from Huckleberry Park, which has slides and a picnic table."

"It certainly sounds like a locale that menacing bad guys would choose as their hideout."

I ran a search for castles in the area and didn't come up with anything for that either. "Let me see the key."

Willard eyed me, and I thought she would object, but she drew it from a zipper pocket and slid it across the map. "Why?"

I took a picture of it. "To see if anything comes up on a reverse image search."

"Not a bad idea."

"I can see you're warming up to me."

"Like a blowtorch to scrap metal."

I looked at the captain as the search ran. "I'm the scrap metal in that metaphor, right?"

He nodded. "I think so."

"It's a simile, Thorvald." Willard pointed at a brown patch of land adjacent to our forest-service road. "Look at this."

The topography lines put it on the top of a hill about halfway down the road. I tried to remember if I'd noticed that spot during my drive, but I mostly remembered walls of trees to either side of the road.

Willard glanced at Rodriguez. "I don't remember any open areas like this, do you?"

"No, ma'am."

"Thorvald, did you and your night vision see any clearings?"

"No, but it's possible that trees along the road could have blocked it from our view."

"Maybe." Willard sounded doubtful. "Look at the topo lines though. That's a hundred feet above that road we were on. Even if there were trees, we should have seen a hill through them."

"There were *lots* of hills," I said. "And a hundred feet isn't that high. Not necessarily above the trees."

"I don't see a castle on top of it." Rodriguez pointed to the bare spot.

"Maybe that was recently constructed." Willard started looking for the date of the map.

I scanned the results of my image search and found a lot of metal bookmarks vaguely shaped like our key but no exact matches. It had been a long shot.

"Here's your salad, Miss." One of the cooks had brought it out this time, but he appeared as flummoxed as the waitress had been about where to put it. "Where would you like it?"

"Miss?" Rodriguez's eyes crinkled as he mouthed this.

Willard gave him a dark look.

"I'll take it. Thank you." Willard took the plate and set it on the floor beside her.

The cook gaped and appeared aggrieved, but Willard turned her *look* on him.

"You're welcome, ma'am." He hurried back to the kitchen.

"I like how you were escalated from miss to ma'am after you glared at him, ma'am." Rodriguez's eyes crinkled even more.

"I think he just noticed that I was older than he thought."

"Or you oozed military authority at him."

Willard shook her head and pointed at a date in the margin. "The map is seven years old."

I opened a Google map of the area on my phone and zoomed in to try to find the corresponding bald spot. The web map didn't have topography lines, so I had to do my best to match it by the bends in the road. "I don't see that cleared place on this map. It's all green along our road."

"What's the date on that one?"

"Ah… The imagery is from last year."

"If it was logged, maybe it's grown back," Rodriguez said.

"Trees don't grow back in six years. Not even if the area was replanted. And this looks like it was clear-cut." Willard put her finger on the map on the table. "There wasn't anything there when this was made. There *still* shouldn't be much there."

"But there is." I showed them my map.

"Let's take a trip back out there and wave the key at the area." Willard's phone rang.

I dropped a pin onto the location on my map so I could get directions to the precise place. I sucked in a breath. One Cave Misty Loop Lane came up on the map as a location slightly to the side of my pin.

When I showed Willard, she nodded, but her face was grim, and she seemed focused on the call. I hadn't been trying to listen in.

"Send me the address," she said. "I'll send Captain Rodriguez over."

His eyebrows rose.

"Another body," Willard said as she hung up. "Mauled by a tiger. Here." She pointed to a housing development near the shore of Lake Whatcom. As the crow flew, it wasn't that far from our address, but I already knew they were more than a half hour drive apart, thanks to the roughness of those roads. "The police are there, but they want someone from our office to take a look. That means they suspect something otherworldly at work."

"More otherworldly than giant tiger claws?" I asked.

"Must be. They've seen a number of bodies killed by those this week."

"You don't think we should both go, ma'am?" Rodriguez frowned. "It's not that far out of the way."

"No, because I can already tell Thorvald is going directly to this suspicious spot on Misty Loop Lane, and I'm not letting her tramp around out there without supervision."

"Supervision?" I mouthed, not bothering to deny the rest. With Michael and the sickly cub on my mind, I had no intention of delaying.

"Couldn't you just take the key from her?" Rodriguez clearly didn't want to let his superior wander off into the woods alone—or alone with the unpredictable and *maverick* me.

"You could try." I smiled tightly at them and slid it into my pocket.

CHAPTER 13

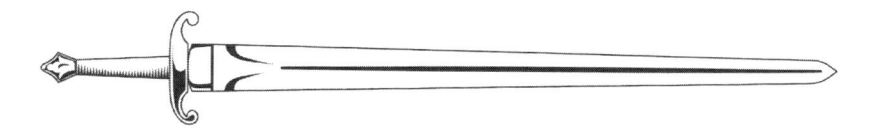

A S MICHAEL AND I WALKED out of Quinn's Pub on Capitol Hill, my stomach pleasantly full of chimichurri steak and wild boar sloppy joe fries, he brought up the subject I'd been expecting him to broach all night.

"What do you think about living together, Val?"

We were holding hands—he'd gotten used to walking on my left for this, so I could draw Fezzik quickly from the thigh hol ster on my right—and he smiled and squeezed my fingers.

"On your boat with the bed in the cupboard?" As always, I kept my eyes open and my senses alert as we walked.

Night had fallen while we were eating, and we'd parked on a back street that wasn't well lit. I wasn't wearing my sword today—sitting down with it in restaurants was awkward—but I was always ready for a fight.

Nobody had tried to shoot me in the past few weeks, and that made me uneasy. It was only a matter of time. I expected one or more of the trolls from the dead thief's family to come after me, though any number of the other enemies I'd made over the years might try too. Being out in the open in the city wasn't that smart, but as Michael was always quick to point out, I had to eat.

"I'd be happy to have you there," he said, "but I was thinking of your apartment. Or I could sell the boat, and maybe we could go in together on a house."

Sell the boat? I looked at him. Damn, he was serious.

Was I *that serious? These past months that we'd gone from friends to lovers had been enjoyable, and I'd liked having someone I could talk business with, but I always worried about letting myself get too close to people, people who could be hurt by my life. It seemed a weakness that I'd allowed myself this relationship, an indulgence that I would regret later, but I'd been lonely since my divorce and since leaving the army, where I'd had colleagues to talk to and work with. Freelance assassins, as I'd learned, worked alone.*

"It's probably not a good idea."

"Ah." He didn't sound surprised, but he did sound disappointed.

"Not because I don't care about you and like being with you." *That was the problem. I did.* "I'm just dangerous to be around."

"Like a gremlin at midnight, huh?" He managed a fleeting smile.

"You know what I mean."

"I do, but I've also chosen a life that could get me killed one day."

"Is that supposed to be comforting?"

We crossed a street at an intersection, and I veered to avoid walking directly under the halo of a streetlight on the corner. It would have left us illuminated to any enemies out there.

"It just means that even if I didn't know you, I could get myself in trouble. I'm willing to risk—"

As we continued along the sidewalk, my senses twanged at the rapid approach of magical beings. Trolls. Two of them. They were coming from the cross street toward the intersection we had just passed through.

"Trouble's coming now." *I released Michael's hand, foisted my keys into his grip, and pushed him toward the Jeep.* "Get in the car and stay down. Hurry."

Michael hesitated, but only for a second. He knew me well enough not to question me about trouble, and he rushed in the direction I'd pointed.

Meanwhile, I sprang onto steps in an alcove that led up to double doors leading into a brick apartment building.

I thought about running inside, but the trolls were only seconds from rounding the corner, and I didn't want them to mistakenly go after Michael. Or intentionally.

After tapping my camouflage charm, I drew Fezzik and leaned far enough out of the alcove to take aim. The trolls slowed down before they came into view. The whispers of a conversation in their language reached my ears, and I activated my translation charm.

"...disappeared."

"She's got magic that hides her. She's still there."

"Shh, she's listening."

Yes, I was. Listening and waiting.

I eyed the alcove, suspecting I would end up fighting from it. There wasn't much besides a couple of bicycles chained in a rack beside the stairs. The sign for the building dangled from two chains above my head. Maybe I could use it to climb up the wall and to the roof, then cut diagonally across the top of the building and jump down behind the trolls.

Before I could turn consideration to action, my enemies rushed around the corner. The two huge blue-skinned trolls wore trench coats and hats and carried automatic firearms, huge belts of ammunition dangling from them.

Since I knew they were after me, I didn't hesitate to shoot. The cracks of my pistol rang out, and bullets slammed into their chests. But the rounds thudded against armor instead of piercing flesh.

The trolls opened fire, and I ducked back into the alcove. Bullets tore into the entryway, chips of brick and mortar pelting my cheek.

Their gunfire came as rapid as drumbeats in a heavy-metal song, and I sensed the trolls advancing to my position behind the fire. They couldn't see me, couldn't know if I was trying to flee the alcove, but they were spraying the cement and the air above it to cut down on any chance of escape. Rounds hammered into cars parked along the street, and I hoped Michael had found cover.

I ran up the stairs and sprang from the top one into the air, leaping five feet to catch the iron sign dangling above the steps. It wanted to sway riotously under my weight, but I twisted and adjusted, stilling it—not that the trolls would hear the chains creaking over all the noise they were making. Then I leaned out, dangling from one arm while I aimed Fezzik with the other.

The trolls didn't anticipate me at that height and were focusing their fire at ground level. I fired twice. Their faces weren't in view from that height, but I had no trouble targeting their heads. My bullets slammed into their skulls, and I fired several more rounds. It was unlikely they wore armor under their hats, but troll skulls were thick.

One dropped his rifle and toppled to the sidewalk. Though hit, the other didn't fall immediately. He jerked his rifle up toward me.

An instant before he fired, I leaned back and dropped down to the bottom step. His bullets tore into the sign as he reached the alcove. Landing soundlessly, I fired from a crouch. This time, I took him in the eye.

He slumped, joining his buddy on the ground. All shots ceased, replaced by the wail of a police siren heading this way.

I left the trolls for them to deal with and didn't deactivate my stealth charm until I reached the Jeep. Even though other cars had been parked between it and the trolls, it had still taken bullets to the back corner. But I was more worried about Michael.

He stepped out from where he'd been crouched between the front bumper of the Jeep and the back of the next car. That car had lost its rear window to bullets, the glass shattered in twin spiderwebs.

"That was noisy trouble." Michael smiled, and I rushed forward to hug him, but his eyes were tight with tension—or pain?—and he was gripping his side through his jacket.

"Did you get shot?"

"Just a little. That all happened faster than I expected." He opened his jacket, and there was just enough light to see blood staining his side under his ribs. "And I admit I may have been looking out because I was worried for you and wanted to find a way to help. I should have known you could handle it."

I hugged him, careful not to touch him close to the wound. "Let's get you to the hospital."

"My first gunshot wound, and it wasn't even for finding a priceless treasure. Disappointing."

I guided him toward the passenger seat. "Let's hope it's your last gunshot wound."

I was too amped up from the fight to cry, but I knew I would later. Exactly what I'd feared would happen had happened. I tried to tell myself that it could have been worse—he was still smiling and making jokes—but it didn't help.

The memory faded as I turned off the paved road and onto the muddy, barely discernible Misty Loop Lane. It didn't surprise me that thoughts of that night had reared up in my mind. Not only was Michael in danger but I was, once again, knowingly heading into trouble with a mundane human being who didn't have magical blood to help her survive against stronger enemies. She didn't even have any magical weapons. Being able to shoot Hawkeye at the range only mattered if one's foe was susceptible to bullets.

The Jeep hit a pond-sized puddle and sprayed muddy water high enough to spatter the windshield. A grunt came from the back seat as we tilted and lurched before powering up the far side of the depression.

I glanced in the rearview mirror. I'd been surprised that Willard had agreed to ride with me—though she and the captain only had one vehicle between them, so she hadn't had much choice—and even more surprised when she'd agreed to sit in the back because, as I'd told her, "The cub's been riding shotgun."

"I feel like it's been weeks since I've seen the sun," I said, thinking we should try to establish a rapport before walking into battle together.

Aside from that, even if I was more worried about Michael than my next paycheck, it kept crossing my mind that I would have to tighten my belt considerably if I didn't get any government gigs going forward. Even if Willard only threw me an assignment a few times a year, it would help out. I just had to convince her that I was good enough and reliable enough to hire.

"Tell me about it. My last duty station was in Texas." That was the first bit of personal information she'd shared.

"This is a slightly different climate."

"Slightly."

We plowed through another deep puddle. The road wasn't any less bumpy and pothole-filled the second time down it. Dawn had come while we'd been in the restaurant, but the fog was so thick that it scarcely mattered.

I searched for something useful to share with a newcomer to the area. "If you decide to grow tomatoes, do the cherry or grape ones.

You'll thank me. Now and then, we get a nice sunny summer, but more often, it's still rainy through Fourth of July."

There, that was what normal people talked about besides the weather, right? Never mind that my gardening efforts were sporadic and sad because I traveled so often for work. It was only because of my elven heritage and a fondness for tomatoes that every third or fourth year, I attempted to grow some on my balcony.

"I don't garden," Willard said.

"Too busy hurling weights around?"

"Sometimes, I hurl nosy assassins around too."

I quirked an eyebrow toward her reflection in the mirror. "You could try."

We went over a bump, and she cursed and flexed her fingers around the oh-shit handle. "Happily."

I glanced at my phone's map. Less than two miles to the spot where I'd stuck my tack, but there were a lot of bends and potholes between here and there.

"Fall gives us some pretty good autumn foliage," I said, taking another stab at rapport-building.

"Is this what you talked about with Colonel Hobbs? Cherry tomatoes and pretty leaves?"

"Yeah, he was a real poetical man."

"His record says he's a Green Beret."

"Are they not allowed to be poetical?"

"It's not encouraged."

Willard would probably take it as a compliment if I told her she was more of a hard-ass than Hobbs had been.

She rolled down the back window. "Your car smells, Thorvald."

"The last time I had a mission that took me out of town, I had to hike off after someone in the mountains, and it took a few days. While I was gone, a raccoon got in and feasted on the food rations I'd left inside. And then he did what raccoons do after he feasted. I've cleaned it a few times, but the back is still somewhat fragrant. I'm thinking of getting an air freshener."

"Fantastic." She grunted again when I drove through a particularly deep pothole. "Any chance you'd let *me* drive?"

"No. But I'm surprised you didn't insist on riding up front."

"Your fanged buddy is up there."

"She's sleeping."

"She wasn't in the medical examiner's office. She was interested in that body."

"So?"

"She didn't look scared by whatever she smelled on it."

I considered that. Would a weaker predator shy away from a body mauled by a stronger predator? I wasn't sure it worked that way in the animal world. Critters always seemed to give things a good long sniff, no matter what had happened.

"Were *you* scared?" I asked.

"I have a healthy respect for things with claws longer than my fingers, and whatever did that looked like it might qualify."

"True."

I glanced at the map again. "We're almost there."

"Good. You going to leave the cat in the car?"

"I think so. She helped me find some ogres with a hidden camp, but she did it by running away from me and into their camp, where things could have turned ugly if they'd managed to catch her. Besides, this is more than sleep." I leaned over and rested a hand on the cub's soft furry side, but she didn't stir. "She's been getting quieter and quieter. Like I said, I think she needs to go back to her realm, but I don't know how to send her."

We reached the bend in the road that we'd studied on the map. In person, it was as unremarkable as before.

Thanks to the fog, the gray daylight didn't make it any easier to see into the brush. The hill Willard had pointed out on the map could have been just off to the side of the road, and I never would have known. An entire mountain could have been there.

I pulled out the metal key artifact. It seemed faintly warm, but I couldn't tell if that was a hint that we were close to whatever door it unlocked, or if my own body heat had warmed it in my pocket.

When I stepped out of the Jeep, the fog wreathed my legs so densely that I couldn't see my boots. I grabbed my weapons and walked around to the other side of the vehicle to peer into the woods, both with my eyes and with my sixth sense. According to the map, the cleared-and-then-not-cleared hilltop should be to the south.

The damp air smelled of wet foliage and decaying leaves. I sniffed for the scent of a fire burning or anything else that might have suggested someone lived out here. But I didn't smell, see, or sense anything out of the ordinary.

Until a distant roar rolled through the forest, the eerie not-quite-natural sound lifting the hairs on my arms.

"Cougars don't roar," Willard noted.

"If it's the same feline that mauled that person, it's had a busy well-traveled night."

"If it really is a tiger—and nobody's survived being visited by it yet, so we don't know—normal ones will travel ten to twenty miles to hunt in a night. I don't know about magical ones." Willard checked her rifle before pulling her pack out of the Jeep and slinging it over her shoulders.

"Is this the portion of the trip where you regale me by reciting encyclopedia entries?"

"The tiger is the largest extant cat species in the world, can weigh up to six hundred and sixty pounds, can leap thirty feet in a single jump, can eat eighty-eight pounds of meat in a day, and prefers to sneak up on its prey and ambush it from hiding." Willard eyed the mist-blanketed woods around us. Hiding spots were aplenty.

"Consider me regaled. What's extant mean?"

"Not extinct. Don't you read any books when you're not busy killing people?"

"Of course. I just finished a re-read of *The Last Unicorn*."

"That's a kids' book."

"It's a classic for children of all ages." As I slid a fresh magazine into Fezzik, I decided not to mention that I owned the entire Harry Potter collection in hardback.

A clack came from behind me, and I jumped, my heart rate springing to double-time as I imagined tigers ambushing us from the trees. It took me a moment—and another clack—to realize it was the cub pawing at the window. Intent green eyes regarded me through the glass.

"Your cat either wants to come with us or has to pee," Willard remarked.

"I don't think she does that." Though I was hesitant to let her out, lest she run off and get in trouble again, I also didn't want her to destroy the Jeep if I kept her in there against her wishes. Aside from my love for intact seatbelts, I had to consider that we might need to make a fast getaway later.

"Then she truly is magical. I have a cat, and her litter box needs changing regularly."

It was hard to imagine Willard cuddling up to some pet at night. Though some house cats were aloof and independent, so maybe that was a perfect fit for her.

"Does that mean you need to hurry home ASAP to clean it?" I asked.

"The neighbor is watching her, but yes. She's a vocal handful, and I have to pay handsomely to get people to take care of her."

The cub clacked her claws against the window again.

"A handful, huh?" I opened the door so my furry princess could bound down into the mud. She splatted a paw into it, spraying murky water onto my jeans. "Hard to imagine."

"Pets are demanding." Willard almost smiled.

Maybe cats were the thing we would bond over out here.

She pointed into the tall trees to the south. "The hill should be that way."

The roar of the tiger drifted to us again—from the south.

"Goody."

"Tigers are also supposed to be nocturnal," Willard said. "Maybe we'll get lucky, and it's bedding down for the day."

The gray sky above us, only vaguely visible through the fog, barely fit the definition of daylight. I doubted even a vampire would be forced indoors at this level of illumination.

The cub headed into the woods. To the south.

"It's moderately disturbing that your cub is eager to unite or reunite with the killer that's making that noise," Willard said.

"It's possible she's on the trail of something else."

"I doubt it."

"Let's hope the killer, if it truly is a feline, will think kindly of us for walking with one of its own kind." I grabbed the backpack I'd used to carry the cub earlier, in case she got tired and wanted a ride.

"Considering that tigers see primates as delicious meals, that seems optimistic."

The cub paused, her silver glow visible in the fog, and looked back at me. Waiting?

"Are you going to lead us to the right spot?" I closed the door softly, afraid sound would travel in the still night.

"Merow?"

"Are you going to lead us to our deaths?" Willard asked.

"Merow?" The cub turned, tail swishing behind her, and trotted deeper into the woods.

"Comforting," Willard said.

I shook my head and followed the cub. Even though Willard's description had reminded me how badass tigers were—and magical tigers were presumably more so—I was more worried about the enemy we didn't yet know. A *tiger* hadn't been the one to order Michael kidnapped.

CHAPTER 14

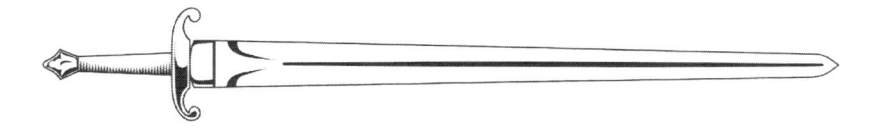

THE CUB LED US THROUGH the trees, stopping frequently to wait for us. Between the tangled undergrowth, moss-carpeted logs, and the perpetual fog, we couldn't advance as quickly and quietly as we would have liked, but Willard didn't slow me down, nor was she any louder than I. Usually, my half-elven feet lent me an advantage when it came to stealth and agility, but she must have had more than intelligence training in her years in the army.

We were both slow compared to the cub. She'd gotten a second wind when she'd jumped out of the Jeep, though the way she flopped down on her side whenever she was waiting for us to catch up worried me. Her aura, which I relied upon to track her, had grown less noticeable in the time we'd been together. Weaker.

When a magical being died, its aura disappeared. I tried not to think about that happening.

A howl floated through the woods, the sound of a wolf's call. Another wolf answered it from the other direction.

They were on either side of us, perhaps a half mile away, though the intervening trees and sound-muting fog made it hard to be certain. The same fog made it difficult to tell if there were any prints out here besides those of small animals. It bothered me that we hadn't found a road or at least a trail heading to this hilltop. If ogres had truly come this way, with Michael draped over one of their shoulders, they should have left signs of their passing.

"Wolves *and* tigers," Willard muttered. "Misty Loop Lane is a damn menagerie."

"Don't forget the ogres and the castle." I let my free hand stray to the pocket where I'd tucked the key. Did it seem warmer than it had at the road? I wasn't positive.

"I haven't. Are we still following the cub? I can't see or hear her."

"She's just ahead. I sense her."

Willard didn't comment on my claim, but if she'd been working in the office long enough to become well versed in the magical, she would know magical beings could sense magic.

Up ahead, the trees thinned, and a path finally came into view. As we stepped onto it, a zap of energy raced along my nerves, and the hair on the back of my neck stood up.

"Did you feel that?" I whispered as Willard joined me.

"No."

The cub sat in the path, as if waiting for us to decide which way to go. I wished I knew. We couldn't see even twenty feet down it either way. I checked the map on my phone to verify what my sense of direction was telling me, that it ran roughly parallel to the road rather than inward like a driveway.

Wolves howled again, closer this time. And more than two of them. They sounded like they were on the path and heading toward us.

"I think we might have crossed a border and stepped on a magical tripwire," I said.

Another howl came from down the path in the opposite direction. The sound of heavy breathing floated across the forest. There was no doubt that the wolves were coming.

"Back to back." Willard lifted her rifle, tucking the stock into the hollow of her shoulder, and turned to face in one direction.

"Right." I drew Fezzik and pointed it in the other direction.

Had I been alone, I would have used my charm to camouflage myself, but that would have left them all focusing on Willard. I also would have opted for Chopper, since the sword wouldn't make noise and announce our arrival to everyone within two miles, but maybe it didn't matter. Whoever had set that magical tripwire knew we were here.

A touch at my shin distracted me. The cub was resting her paw on my legs, claws retracted, and looking up at me with concerned green eyes.

I bent and swooped her up and put her into my pack. There was just enough time to level Fezzik again as the first set of eyes came into view. They glowed like red beacons in the fog, and my senses told me that the approaching wolves were magical.

"Firing," Willard said, a second before she did.

Would her weapon do anything against magical foes? I didn't know.

I aimed right between the eyes streaking toward me as the furry black canine solidified in the fog. More than twice the size of a natural wolf, it jumped as the weapon cracked, somehow anticipating my shot. My bullet sailed under it.

It thudded into another creature behind it that wasn't as fast. A second set of eyes blinked out, but only for a second. The wolf never cried out, and they kept coming.

Behind me, Willard fired rapidly. I did the same, crouching in case I had to spring aside.

My bullets rained into the chests of the two wolves I could see, Fezzik recoiling with each shot, the power comforting in my palm. They tried to dodge or jump over my attacks, but now I knew to expect their speed and anticipated it. My rounds parted thick fur and thudded into flesh and bone. But the unnatural wolves kept coming. The red eyes seemed to flare brighter, angrier.

"My bullets aren't stopping them," Willard said, her tone calm but the words clipped and tense.

"I know. I'm switching to my sword."

There was no time to say more. As I holstered Fezzik and drew Chopper, the lead wolf sprang for me.

Not wanting to bump Willard with my swings, I rushed forward to meet it. The magical blade flared blue, as if it was hungry for a fight.

The otherworldly wolf had to weigh three hundred pounds, and my instincts screamed at me to slash at the snapping jaws, anything to keep the fangs away from my neck, but I needed to strike a more vital target.

As I dodged its attack, the unaccustomed weight of the cub rocking on my back and almost upsetting my balance, I plunged my blade in under its jaws. The tip sank into the fur of its throat, and I thought it would be a killing blow.

But its head whipped around, still snapping at me as the wolf landed. I skittered back, branches clawing at my pack and the cub screeching a protest. It charged again, jaws opening wide, and I braced myself. I swung Chopper toward its gleaming fangs, and metal screeched against teeth, slicing into its tongue. The wolf shook its head, giving me the opening I needed. I swung Chopper in hard enough to cut through its skull and into its brain.

For the first time, one of the wolves yelped and cried out. It dropped to the ground, half disappearing in the fog as the body went limp.

The second wolf lunged at me before I could celebrate any victory. With little room to maneuver on the path, I backed up again. Fortunately, Willard had moved off to the side, using two trees to protect her flanks, and wasn't in my way. She was keeping her two wolves busy so they couldn't get through to my back.

As my second wolf tramped over the first in its eagerness to get to me, I lunged back in to meet its snapping jaws with a thrust from my sword. Power seemed to flow out of Chopper and into the wolf. It yelped as the tip of the blade sank into its chest. The eyes flared brighter red, then went dark.

I yanked my blade free, made sure I didn't sense any more coming down the path, and spun to help Willard. Somehow, even with her mundane rifle, she'd managed to down one of her fanged foes. Another huge gray wolf was snapping at her with berserker-like fury. She fired until she ran out of bullets, then ducked behind one of the trees to reload.

The wolf lunged after her, not paying attention to me. I rushed at its flank and swung down with Chopper like a logger splitting wood. The blade sliced through fur and flesh—and vertebrae.

Our foe yowled, and its back legs collapsed, but that didn't keep it from trying to spin and go after me. I pulled my blade free and scooted out of its range. As I prepared to lunge in again, Willard whistled. Snarling, the wolf twisted back toward her. She stepped out from behind the tree and shot it in one of its glowing red eyes. It slumped lifeless to the ground.

"Thanks for the help," she said.

"You're welcome." While I wiped my blade, I reached out with my senses to see if any more magical creatures were in the area.

"I found out I had to shoot them exactly in the eye for my bullets to do anything. More than once." Willard pointed at the first one she'd killed. "I took that one in the right eye three times in a row. There have to be three bullets lined up back to back in its brain."

"They're magical wolves."

She gave me a sarcastic look. "You think?"

"I wasn't sure if you were confused as to why a mundane rifle didn't work that well."

"Less confused and more wondering where I should go to buy one like yours. Though I noticed even you switched." Willard considered Chopper, the blade still glowing as I finished wiping off the blood.

"There's a lady in town with gnomish blood who makes magical firearms. Her name is Nin. She runs the Crying Tiger food truck."

"I've heard of her. I'll check it out."

"Get the beef and rice while you're there. It's good."

"Is that where you got that sword too?"

"No. I won this in battle a few years back." I sheathed Chopper carefully, the cub still in the pack also occupying room on my back.

"Does that mean you looted it off your enemy after you killed it?" Willard sounded judgmental, as if her unit's basement wasn't full of magical artifacts that the agents had brought back after defeating enemies.

"Yes, but it was a zombie lord menacing the locals by raising the dead from a cemetery. I didn't think anyone would object."

"It looks dwarvish. How did the zombie lord get it?"

"We didn't discuss it while we were fighting. My guess is that he looted it from one of *his* enemies after killing him." I frowned at her, prepared to argue further that it was rightfully mine, but Willard was now gazing up and to the south.

The fog had thinned, and the hill we'd only seen on the map had come into view. If it had truly been clear-cut once, there wasn't evidence of it now. The trees had grown back in a hurry and stretched as tall as they did elsewhere in the forest. Still, it looked like the very top of the hill might be more open.

"I believe that's our hill," Willard said, then waved for me to follow her over one of the wolf bodies and up the path.

After only a few steps, she pointed her rifle down at the mud. A huge five-toed barefoot print was visible—that of an ogre. It had come from the direction of the road and walked along the path in the direction that looked like it led to the hill.

"But where's our castle?" I asked.

"Maybe it's a *small* castle."

"Maybe that'll make it easier to storm." I thought of my keychain.

"I doubt it. You still have the key?"

I tapped my pocket to make sure the magical item hadn't fallen out. "Yes."

"Good. Are you leading or am I?" Willard looked at the cub when she said it, not me.

I glanced back as the cub rested her chin on my shoulder.

"I think I'm leading," I said, wondering if she had grown too weary or had lost interest. And if the latter, why?

Shaking my head, I followed the ogre prints up the path. We would find out one way or another soon.

I'm coming for you, Michael, I thought, hoping the castle was up there, and that he was in it and all right.

CHAPTER 15

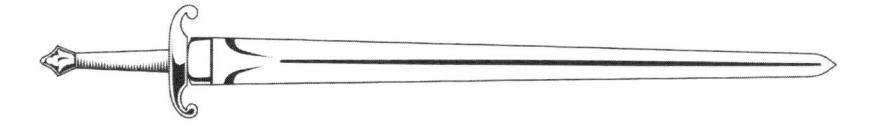

THE HILLTOP WAS EMPTY, SAVE for ribbons of fog curling through the grass and around the occasional stump.

We crouched to the side of the muddy path, hiding behind the last trees and ferns before the forest opened up into the grass. Fog stretched away in all directions, this hilltop an island amid gray. The path continued out into the grass, though from our vantage point, it appeared to continue on and down the other side. But wolves and magical tripwires wouldn't have been placed to guard an empty hilltop.

I slipped what we believed was a magical key out of my pocket. Before, I'd thought it slightly warm. Now, there was no doubt. It heated my palm noticeably in the cool damp air.

"If you're a key, where's the lock?" I rubbed the castle emblem with my thumb. Nothing happened. I waved it in the air. Nothing happened. I clunked it against the nearest tree.

Willard's eyebrows twitched as she watched, but she didn't comment. "Any ideas?"

She started to reply, but I was holding it over my shoulder for the cub to look at.

Willard snorted. "Is she the brains in this outfit?"

"I don't know. She hasn't recited any encyclopedias to me yet."

The cub licked the castle emblem.

"Ew." I pulled it away and wiped it off.

While I was distracted doing that, Willard sucked in a breath and gripped my arm. She was staring at the hilltop.

A structure was slowly appearing in the fog, a rambling structure with several levels, including crenelated parapets stretching between towers with spires. The whole thing was made from wood, predominantly intact logs, and it made me think of some Colonial army fort rather than a castle. But the structure radiated magic, so I had little doubt that this was our place. That magic wasn't as powerful as what I sensed from Chopper, but there was a lot of it. At the least, I suspected wards or alarms to alert those inside of intruders.

I looked down at our key, wondering if the cat licking it had evoked its magic or if rubbing it had done the trick.

"It's made of logs," Willard said, sounding even more bemused by the structure than I was. "I don't think you can call it a castle if it's made out of logs."

"Why don't we go knock on the door and discuss it with the owner?" I waved at double doors made from split logs behind a portcullis also made from wood. The muddy path now led to a drawbridge that was down over a meandering moat that had appeared along with the structure.

"I *should* knock and show them my warrant." Willard didn't rise to do so. She was eyeing the windows in the towers. Looking for guards? Wondering if she would be shot as she walked up?

"Do you *have* a warrant?"

"Yeah. For One Cave Misty Loop Lane."

"I wonder if there's actually a cave anywhere." Earlier, I'd jokingly wondered if something had been lost in translation when the ogre scrivener had recorded that address. Now, it occurred to me that the thought might have been more accurate than I'd suspected. If ogres all lived in caves, maybe they used that word for all dwellings.

Willard shook her head. "I don't care. I just want to end the murders. We're getting to the bottom of this bloodthirsty tiger, and we're finding Kwon. *Today*."

This wasn't the time to get emotional, but it touched me that she'd added finding Michael to her mission.

Willard stood up, but I held out a hand to stop her. "Are you really thinking of knocking?"

"And showing them the warrant, yes. Even if I'm skeptical that the owners of this place are property-tax-paying citizens, I have to proceed legally and professionally. There are rules and procedures." Willard gave me a flat look, as if to say she doubted I paid attention to such things.

She wasn't wrong. A part of me wanted to set up my phone to film what would likely be a ludicrous encounter, but a larger part of me knew a stealthy incursion would be better. Though maybe it was silly to believe we could enter stealthily. We'd killed their wolves and made a lot of noise doing it. Whoever lived here knew we were coming.

Unfortunately, even though I could sense the magic of the structure itself, I couldn't detect anything or anyone inside. The walls blocked my senses as well as my eyesight. Inside, there could be one dangerous guy... or a hundred. The log castle was large enough to hold an army.

"Why don't you do that," I suggested, "while I climb up a tower and sneak in through a window?"

"While you've got that charm activated?"

"Yes."

"Would you be able to skulk around inside without leaving mud and puddles on the floor?"

"I'll wipe my boots on the crenellations before I go in."

Willard shrugged. "You don't work for me, so I can't tell you what to do. But I'll assume you want me to keep them distracted for as long as possible."

"I'd appreciate that. Also, don't get shot. Or eaten by a tiger."

"I had no idea you cared."

"I don't, but I'd feel obligated to carry you out over my shoulder, and you look heavier than this cub."

"I'm barely one-fifty. If you can't do a fireman carry on me, I'm going to send a personal trainer to your door after this."

"Better than the trolls and orcs who usually show up." I grimaced, memories of the time Michael had been shot by trolls fresh in my mind. Shaking my head, I pulled out my phone. "Give me your number in case I need to text you."

I had one bar of reception. Hopefully that would be enough.

"Here." Willard pulled out her own phone and sent me a text without asking for my number.

"You already put me in your contacts list? We're destined to be besties. Maybe we should start practicing our fist bumps."

"Or maybe we should deal with the people in that castle." Willard waved at me and stepped back out onto the path.

"Wait." I gave her two of the grenades I'd gotten from Nin. "Just in case they don't want to talk to you."

Willard considered them, nodded with approval, then slipped them into an outer pocket of her pack. "Thanks."

I would win her over yet.

As I tapped my cloaking charm and hopefully disappeared from the senses of the castle owner, Willard pulled a folded stack of papers out from another pocket. She truly did have a warrant. I would have laughed, but I was too busy sneaking away.

Assuming the drawbridge had alarms or traps, I thought about swimming or trying to run and jump across the moat. A pair of alligators swam past, beady eyes and the tips of their snouts visible above the water, and I ditched that idea. My charm would keep them from seeing or smelling me, but it didn't stifle sound, and it would be hard to swim without making noise.

A hint of magic came from harnesses around their torsos, probably some compulsion that kept them from fleeing the chilly northwest and going south to a climate more appropriate for them.

There were iron bands around the logs of the drawbridge, and I also sensed magic radiating from them. Alarms? Instead of investigating further, I stepped over them. The portcullis was raised halfway, as if in invitation.

Willard could accept that invitation. I skirted the castle wall and jogged along the one-foot-wide grassy ledge between it and the moat. Another set of alligators swam past, and the cub offered a questioning, "Merow?"

"Shh," I breathed.

Their beady black eyes turned in my direction. I ran faster, going as quickly as I could without making noise.

When I was around the corner of the castle and out of sight of the main entrance, I picked a spot to climb up the wall. Having extra furry weight on my back made it more difficult than usual, but I found sufficient hand- and footholds among the bumpy logs and made it the fifteen feet to the top.

A true castle would have had a courtyard to go along with the parapet and towers, but the interior of the structure was covered with a metal roof. Not seeing any doors or access panels, I headed toward the nearest tower, which also had the nearest window large enough to enter through. I climbed again, found the window locked, and rested my hand on it while willing my lock-picking charm to work.

An interior latch clicked faintly. The circular, wood-paneled room inside was empty, the only motion coming from the dancing flames of a kerosene lantern mounted on a wall. I opened the window carefully, staying to the side in case someone was hiding. These looked like guard towers, so it was hard not to imagine brutes with firearms waiting to maim intruders.

Nothing happened.

A faint knock drifted up to my ears as I pulled myself in. Willard at the front door with her warrant in hand.

I understood why she, an official government representative, felt compelled to obey the law, but I was used to doing things my way and much preferred sneaking in and figuring out what I was dealing with before announcing myself. But if whoever owned the castle focused on her and that kept them from looking for me, all the better. I only hoped Willard didn't get hurt because she was out in the open and an easy target. Based on our brief time together, I had no problem accepting that she was a capable warrior, but she didn't have my array of magical tools and weapons, so that put her at a disadvantage here.

Once I was inside the castle, I could sense the magic that I hadn't been able to detect through the outer wall. And I grimaced at the amount of it. Mostly artifacts—it was hard to tell what they did, but I suspected many were for defending this place—but also beings. At least one ogre and someone else I couldn't quite identify. Someone powerful. I could usually tell someone's species by their aura, but not this time. He or she vaguely reminded me of the nature-tinted auras that I'd been told represented elves, but that wasn't quite right. The aura was darker and more ominous than that. Malevolent.

There were also magical creatures prowling the hallways and rooms of the castle. More of the wolves. Since we'd defeated four of them, I should have been bolstered, but there were a *lot* of them in here. Even with magical weapons, I could only fight so many at a time. I would have to be careful not to be caught out in the open.

Since Michael didn't have magical blood, I couldn't sense if he was here or not. Surprisingly, I didn't sense anything like a grown-up version of the cub either. We'd heard those great feline roars outside but so far hadn't seen or sensed the source of them. Maybe it was a mundane tiger that had been trained to kill, not needing any magical enhancement for the job, and that was why I couldn't detect it.

"Merow?" came a tentative sound from the cub.

I winced. There was no way I could convey to her that we needed to be quiet. Nor could I see a way forward that wouldn't put her at risk.

"I think you better stay here, kid." I eased the pack off my shoulders and pulled the cub out. She sat and looked up at me, green eyes liquid and wan. "I have a feeling I'm going to end up in another fight—or lots of them. I don't want you to get taken out. This is a nice room. Look, there's a weapons rack you can nibble on."

She stood and nibbled on my bootlaces instead.

"Funny." I stroked her back a few times, then plopped her down by the weapons rack. I held my hands up as if I could command her like a dog to stay.

Her sad eyes tracked me as I backed away, and she didn't try to follow me to the door.

"Stay here," I whispered, my throat tight with emotion. "I'll come back for you."

I hoped it wasn't a lie.

As soon as I shut her in the room, my sense of urgency propelled me across a landing and down a set of steps. The ogre and the mysterious being were on the ground floor near the back of the castle, but the hallways all directed me toward the front of the building. It looked like I wouldn't be able to sneak around and come at them from behind.

When I reached the ground floor and peeked out of the stairway, I spotted the first of the roving creatures. Four of the big red-eyed wolves trotted down a hallway, a faded gray carpet keeping their claws from clacking on the wooden floor underneath.

I padded silently back up the stairs several steps and waited for them to pass. As long as I didn't make a noise, they shouldn't sense me through my camouflage charm, but if their route took them up the stairs toward me, they would get close enough to see through the protective magic.

I waited with Chopper in hand. This time, I wouldn't use Fezzik unless I had to, though that might be inevitable if I had to battle four at once. I touched the ammo pouches that held Nin's grenades, half checking to make sure they were still there and half contemplating ways I might throw one to take out the maximum number of enemies.

Two of the wolves trotted past without glancing up, the hulking black forms taking up most of the hallway. The second two paused at the base of the stairs. One looked straight at me, its eyes glowing crimson in halls dimly lit by the wall lanterns. One wolf's nose quivered as it tested the air. I waited with my sword poised.

A faint gray mist curled around the wolves' legs, as if the outside was seeping into the castle. It seemed strange, but I was too focused on the creatures to do more than note it. Long seconds slipped past as the wolf kept sniffing, kept looking in my direction. The one beside him also turned to look up the stairs.

Just as I was certain they knew I was there and would race toward me, both wolves' heads swung back the way they had come. I hadn't heard anything, but all four of the creatures reversed direction and trotted off toward what I guessed was the front door of the place.

Worried they'd heard Willard, I followed after them. At an intersection, I peered down a hallway that looked like it led deeper into the castle—toward the being with the dangerous aura—but the wolves had gone straight toward what appeared to be a large foyer or grand entrance hall. I had to make sure they didn't attack Willard en masse.

As I crept after them, I scanned my surroundings with all of my senses alert. There had to be traps in here. I didn't want to step in one.

When I reached the entrance hall, the area lit by more kerosene lanterns as well as chandeliers hanging from wide beams near the ceiling, I almost forgot about the wolves. Michael lay on his side on the floor, gagged and bruised with his ankles and his wrists tied.

The urge to sprint to him and cut his bonds almost propelled me into the hall, but I'd just been thinking of traps, and my instincts screamed that this was one. The wolves had parted and sat at the four corners of the large room. A wide back hallway headed toward the rear of the castle.

Michael lay in the middle of a rectangular carpet. Walking on it might trigger a trap. I sensed magic emanating from the area. Or was it emanating from him? Next to the carpet, a rusty metal starburst was embedded in the wood floor like a decorative medallion. It also emanated magic.

I frowned at Michael, trying to piece together the puzzle, but his eyes were closed, so he couldn't give me any clues. I could make out his chest expanding and contracting with breaths. He was alive—for now.

But something was off. Was that truly my Michael? Or might it be an illusion? If it was, it was a good one.

I stepped out of the hallway, watching for tripwires, though the strange mist would have made it difficult to see anything small or thin. The air now even had a smell to it, like the damp forest outside, with a hint of something pungent and foreign.

As I drew closer to Michael's form, my senses and instincts grew more certain that something was off. If the wolves hadn't been in the room, I would have tossed a coin at him to see if it passed through.

I stopped at the edge of the carpet, though I could barely see it now. The fog had grown denser, that musty forest scent stronger, something about it making me think of sleep and how tired I was after being up all night.

Between one second and the next, I realized that the fog wasn't some innocent byproduct of the weather but was itself a threat. I backed away, not wanting to leave in case that actually *was* Michael but also certain that I would be in trouble if I stayed in the room.

I stumbled as I backed toward the hallway and gaped down at my feet in betrayal and surprise. I had elven blood; I *never* stumbled.

But abruptly my knee buckled, the weight of my body too much to hold up. Some paralyzing magic was stealing the power from my muscles and tilting me toward the black chasm of unconsciousness.

The wolves heard me stumble. All of their heads swiveled toward me, and they ran in my direction.

I could barely keep my fingers wrapped around Chopper's hilt. There was no way I could fight them, not now. I dug into my ammo pouch and pulled out a grenade as I willed my legs to carry me back into the hallway. If there was any chance that was Michael, I couldn't risk bringing the roof down on him. I had to get farther away first.

Though I wanted to retreat all the way to the stairs, I only made it two steps into the hall before my legs gave way completely. I dropped to my knees, my hip banging against the wall, and slid down to the floor.

As the wolves charged into view, I pulled the tab on the grenade and rolled it toward them. It bumped one of their legs and didn't go as far as I wanted.

I tried to pull myself backward, away from the grenade, but my numb hands and legs couldn't even feel the floor beneath me.

My last thought was that this wasn't how I wanted to go out. Not only had I failed to redeem my promise to the cub and return to her, but I'd failed to help Michael. I hadn't accomplished *anything* here.

The grenade blew, its explosive charge amplified by magic, and I had the satisfaction of seeing fur and wolf limbs fly before the shockwave hit me and hurled me down the hall.

With my body numb and unresponsive, I couldn't curl into a ball or do anything to protect myself. My head hit the wall, and the unconsciousness I'd been fighting won.

CHAPTER 16

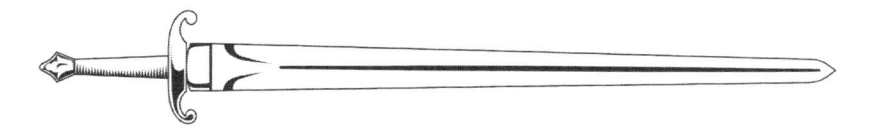

A S SOON AS THEY LET me in, I joined Michael in his hospital room. He smiled at me and seemed in good spirits and fully alert and awake—maybe they'd only had to do a local anesthetic for the bullet removal. I knew from personal experience that bullet extractions were uncomfortable as hell even with numbing agents. I also had the added complication of healing quickly. Normally, that was a good thing, but not if it meant the wound healed around the bullet still lodged inside.

"Sorry about that," Michael said from the bed he was propped up in. "That wasn't how I intended the evening to end."

"That's my line." The bed had rails around it, so I couldn't sit at the foot with him. I pulled up a chair instead. "I'm sorry you were hurt. I should have rushed around the corner and cut them off instead of just telling you to run."

Then he wouldn't have been in the trajectory of any bullets. During his surgery, I'd been sitting in the waiting room and second-guessing my actions that night.

"Right. Because charging big guys with machine guns always goes super well." He waved dismissively. "I had time to get behind your car. If I hadn't been dumb enough to lean out and look, I wouldn't have been hit."

But he'd looked because he'd been worried about me. That made it worse. This was my fault.

"Michael…" I looked down at my hands and plucked at my sleeve.

"Please don't say this proves it would be a bad idea for us to live together. If you're not ready for that, that's fine, but don't let this come between us."

I swallowed, the lump rising in my throat making it hard for me to reply. Not that I knew what to say anyway. I was horrible at this kind of thing. I had feelings, but I never knew how to express them. Even to people I cared about. *Especially* to people I cared about.

"I don't want anything to come between us." I managed to look up and meet his eyes. "But I also don't want you to be hurt again—or worse—because of me. Because we're in a relationship and some enemy of mine figures that out and goes after you. This wasn't even intentional. Think what could happen if…" I lifted my hand but then dropped it. The power to be blunt left me, and I couldn't finish the sentence.

"Like I already said, my life got more dangerous when I chose to involve myself in this underground world of the magical."

"It got a *lot* more dangerous when you chose to involve yourself with me."

"Yeah, but you're worth it." He smiled, but his dark eyes were wary. He feared he'd already lost the argument—lost me.

Seeing that pain in his eyes made me feel like I'd been shot myself. I didn't want to hurt him. And I wished it didn't have to be this way, but me being lonely and liking his company wasn't a good enough reason for me to have a relationship with him, to risk falling in love with him.

Tears pricked at my eyes. Maybe I already had fallen in love. Damn it, when had that happened?

"Thank you, Michael. You're worth a lot too. Everything. But I couldn't live with knowing I'd been responsible for your death."

He slumped back against the pillows. "I guess this means we're not moving in together."

"We couldn't have afforded a house in Seattle anyway."

"Just wait." He forced a smile and pointed at me. "One of these days, I'm going to find a treasure that's going to make me rich."

"I hope so. If you keep getting shot, your health insurance premium is going to go up a lot."

He snorted. "Speaking from experience?"

"Let's just say that being an assassin isn't conducive to a good rate."

Slowly, groggily, I grew aware of rough material scraping along my cheek. It took me a moment to realize that something was wrapped around my ankle like a vise with teeth, and I was being dragged across the carpet. That switched to the cool wood of floorboards and then to something that felt like metal. Somehow, I still gripped my sword hilt, and the blade was being dragged along with me.

My limbs were still numb, but I tried to squeeze my hand tighter, tried to will blood to flow to it and for whatever magic had me paralyzed to wear off.

The pressure around my ankle disappeared, and my senses kicked in, informing me that one of the wolves had been dragging me. I managed to twitch a finger. And then my foot. The creature backed away, leaving me on the metal sunburst floor decoration I'd noticed in the grand hall floor earlier.

I managed to lift my head, turning it enough to see Michael's form on the carpet. He was so close to me now. If I could get the rest of my body working, I could crawl over and check on him.

The floor lurched and shifted underneath me. I tried to roll to the side, but my body was still responding too slowly.

The rays of the sunburst snapped upward, the tips joining to create a pyramid around me—a *cage* around me—leaving only a few gaps that I could see out. Clanks sounded, and a chain descended from the ceiling and hooked to a loop at the top of the pyramid. Somewhere above, a winch creaked, pulling the chain upward. The floor of my cage tilted, and I rolled to one side, cheek pressed to a gap and giving me a view of Michael's form on the carpet.

As the chain pulled me upward, his body faded until it disappeared. I'd been right. It had been an illusion.

Damn it.

The wolves trotted into the hallway in the back—heading off to inform their masters that I'd been captured.

Growling, I forced my jelly-like muscles to work and shoved my way to my knees. That was as far as I could rise, for my head clunked against the slanted sides of my new cage.

Through all of this, I'd managed to keep my hold on Chopper. The magical blade ought to have the power to cut through the thick sunburst bars, even if they were also magical, but only if I could find the room to swing it. My elbow clunked against the side of my cage, making that doubtful.

For the first time, I sensed that the magical auras that I'd noted earlier—the ogre and his mysterious buddy—were on the move. Heading this way. Where I was wrapped up like a present under a Christmas tree.

Snarling, I maneuvered my sword until the tip pressed against one of the gaps and slid it between the rays of the sunburst. Since I couldn't swing it, I sawed the blade back and forth against the bars.

"Thorvald?" came a whisper from below and behind me.

Willard had made it in and stood with her rifle at the mouth of a hall that likely led to the front doors. Having her find me in this predicament was almost as bad as being found by the bad guys.

"Yeah," I reluctantly said. "Don't inhale the fog if you see it."

That fog had dissipated since I'd been captured, so she probably wasn't in danger.

"And don't hang around," I added. "An ogre is coming along with someone else. And..." I grimaced as, for the first time, I sensed an aura similar to that of the cub. Similar to but much stronger and more powerful. Why hadn't I sensed it earlier? "I think the tiger we've been hearing."

Willard walked forward, alternately eyeing the hall entrances and my cage. It was too high off the floor for her to jump and reach the bottom. I kept sawing with my sword, silently apologizing to Chopper for using it as a file.

"They know we're here, right?" Willard stopped a few paces away and looked up to the chain holding my cage.

"They know *I'm* here. Did you knock and show your warrant to one of the wolves?"

"Nobody answered. I had to force the door open."

"How'd you manage?" I sensed the ogre, tiger, and other being getting closer and sawed harder. Nothing dulled Chopper's magical blade, and I was making progress, but I feared it wouldn't be fast enough. "That looked like a stout door."

"Three side kicks, and the bolt snapped. I wasn't going to resort to that, but then I heard an explosion and figured the door breaking wouldn't faze anyone."

"That was me."

"I figured." Willard lifted her rifle and aimed above my cage.

"What are you—"

She fired, her bullet striking the chain. A shudder went through the cage, but it didn't drop to the ground. She fired again and hit the chain dead on.

"There's magic reinforcing it. Here, try mine." I unholstered Fezzik and was about to try to fit it between the bars when I sensed the tiger. Before, it had been walking at the side of the other castle denizens, but now it was coming fast. "Never mind. The tiger's coming. Get out of here."

"I cracked it." Willard fired again, a third bullet striking the chain.

My cage lurched but didn't fall.

The huge silver tiger that was everything I'd feared it would be came into view, powerful legs propelling it into the grand hall. It glowed slightly, the same as the cub. It—he?—had to weigh a thousand pounds. A thousand pounds of pure muscle.

His green eyes locked not on me but on Willard. She lowered her rifle and opened fire on it.

Those bullets wouldn't hurt it; I knew that even before they landed, striking the glowing tiger and deflecting away.

Still stuck on my knees in the cage, I aimed Fezzik through the bars, hoping my enhanced bullets would do more.

But instead of firing, I shouted, "The cub is in the tower!"

Could he understand? Did he care? Were the cub and this large tiger related or completely unrelated?

Those green eyes glanced up at me, but he kept barreling down on Willard. She backed toward the front hallway, firing as she went, but she didn't have time to escape. With no other choice, I opened fire.

My magical bullets bit into his silver hide, and for the first time, he reacted with a flinch and a roar. It reverberated from the walls and made my cage shudder as much as Willard's bullets had.

It seemed a crime to hurt such a magnificent creature, but he was almost under my cage, and I wouldn't be able to target him through the bottom of it. I couldn't let him get to Willard.

My rounds struck his shoulder and flank, and he veered off before he reached her. He rushed into the side hallway I'd originally come from—a hallway with the walls charred and half tumbled in and the ceiling collapsed. Seeing that made me fear for the cub. When I'd thrown that grenade, I had only been thinking of taking out the wolves, not that I might damage the structure of the castle or collapse her tower.

As the tiger disappeared over the rubble and up the stairwell, I crossed my fingers that the tower was still intact. And that the cub was still in there and safe—assuming the tiger had understood and was going up to check on her. He might simply be fleeing my bullets.

Another fear replaced the last. What if the cub, who had been weaker and weaker as the hours progressed, perished, and the tiger walked in and found her dead? If she meant something to him, he might come back down here and risk my magic bullets to tear out my throat.

The ogre that had been taking his time reaching the grand hall ambled out, a wizard's staff the size of a small tree in his large hand. Unlike most ogres, who favored simple fur or hide vests and trousers, he wore a blue robe sewn with sigils that emanated magic. I'd heard of ogre wizards but had never met one. Until now.

He looked around, his broad face faintly puzzled. On a chain around his neck, he wore a single charm that also emanated magic. A cat-shaped charm.

"If you're looking for your tiger," I said, wanting to make sure he focused on me instead of Willard, "he fled after I perforated his hide."

The ogre did indeed focus on me, but instead of leveling that staff in my direction and casting some spell, he stepped to the side to make room for several wolves to enter, along with one more person. The blond elf male with pointed ears wasn't the monstrous figure I expected, but I realized two things right away: he was a vampire, and he was holding Michael by the throat and forcing him to walk out first.

CHAPTER 17

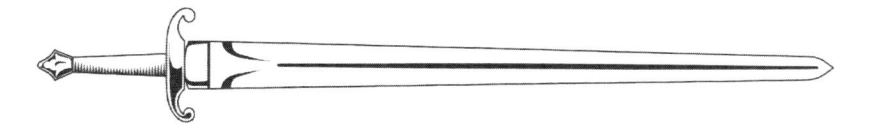

THIS TIME, MICHAEL'S EYES WERE open and pained as they locked onto mine. Bands of invisible but tangible power wrapped around his body like massive cuffs, and he could barely shuffle forward.

I shifted my position in the cramped cage so I could find a gap that I could aim Fezzik through. The cowardly vampire was almost fully behind Michael, but I trusted my aim and knew I could peg him in the forehead if I could find the right angle. Unfortunately, that wouldn't destroy a vampire—it would take a stake to the heart or cleaving his head fully off to do that—but maybe it would jar him into letting Michael go.

This was the real Michael this time, I had no doubt. He struggled against the invisible bonds holding him and shook his head with anger and distress when he saw me.

"Do not," the vampire said in accented English, his voice ringing with power as he lifted a hand. "Do not, *Ruin Bringer*."

The same power that restrained Michael wrapped around me. I'd let Chopper rest on the bottom of the cage while I fired, but now I gripped the hilt and willed the sword to help me repel the attack. The magical grip seemed to lessen, but I could still feel the vampire's hold on me.

The ogre pointed his staff at me, as if it were a bazooka, and loosed a bolt of fiery energy. An instant before it struck the cage, I ducked low.

The metal bars partially deflected the blow, though the cage creaked and rocked ominously, but I caught some of the power. It knocked me against the back of the cage and rattled every tooth in my jaw.

"Do not fight," the vampire repeated. "There is nothing you can do. You were foolish to come with so few allies."

"I tried to round up more people who would be excited to come to your creepy-ass log castle, but the list of interested parties was short."

I glanced out the back of the cage, hoping Willard hadn't been hit by that blow, but she was gone. Good. She would get pulped by these guys. Unfortunately, if I couldn't get out of here, I was in danger of the same.

"Michael, are you all right?"

His jaw was clenched, but it looked like magic held it in place, not his own desire. With effort twisting his face, he wrenched his mouth open to shout, "I'm sorry, Val!"

"Silence." The vampire's hand tightened around his throat, and Michael dropped to his knees.

Fiery rage made me want to tear my cage apart with my bare hands. I fought the power weighing on me and brought Fezzik up to a gap to try to target the bastard without hitting Michael.

"What do you want him for?" I demanded, sweat slithering down the side of my face. I needed the vampire to move a couple of inches…

"I don't want him at all. It's you that I've been trying to lure up here with all manner of bait." The vampire's lip twitched, his elven face handsome even though he was paler than talc. How had an elf been turned into a vampire? Their kind were so long-lived that he couldn't have volunteered because he sought immortality.

"What do you want me for? I'm willing to trade myself for him."

"How noble, but it's not you I particularly care about, though Vroth here has heard of you and would like to kill you."

The ogre smiled and said something in his own language. I was too busy trying to find a way to target the vampire's forehead to worry about going for my translation charm.

"It's your sword that I want," the vampire said.

"My *sword*? You set all this up for my sword? Kidnapping Michael? Sending your tiger out to kill and maim people?"

"Had you scurried up here when Vroth's tiger first started killing people, as we expected, your lover need not have been captured."

I hadn't even *known* about the slayings up here. If Hobbs had still been stationed in Seattle, he would have told me. He would have sent me instead of some other agent.

"But it has given Vroth here time to prove his loyalty and his utility. His tiger even brought me living humans so I could have fresh blood. Human blood is inferior to elven blood, but when you're driven out of your home world, you make do. And you find those who prove themselves useful to you." He reached up to put a hand on the ogre's shoulder. "I have promised to make him a vampire and give him immortality once my goal is achieved."

"Your goal of getting my sword?"

"Indeed." The vampire's smile was icy cold. "Drop it, or your lover dies."

"You'll kill him anyway," I said, though I would trade the sword in a second for Michael's life. If I could be certain the trade offered was a fair one, I would take it, but the last thing I wanted was to give more power to the vampire while his hand was wrapped around Michael's throat.

He shook his head minutely, as if to warn me his captor couldn't be trusted.

"Perhaps," the vampire said. "Perhaps not. I have kept him alive these last days to ensure I had sufficient bait for my trap."

"I need assurances." I slumped, pretending I couldn't resist the power he kept using on me, but I surreptitiously went back to sawing Chopper's blade through the bars. I was more than halfway through one. "I'm willing to make the trade, but you have to let Michael go free and get back to the road. Then you release me from this cage. *Then* I'll give you the sword."

"Of course you will. The Ruin Bringer is so known for being friendly and fair to magical beings."

"I'm not *unfair* to anyone. The only beings I've killed are murderers."

"One society's murderers are another's heroes."

For some reason, I thought of that troll that had been stealing from the meat-packing plant for his people. If he'd *only* stolen, I wouldn't have been sent after him, but he'd been a killer. He'd murdered more than ten people as he stole. *I* wasn't the bad guy here.

"Who considers you a hero, vampire elf?" I demanded, more of the bar filing away under the subtle rasps of my blade. "You just said you were driven out of your world."

"A mistake my people made that I will remedy once I have your sword."

"What's the deal with my sword? It can't possibly be that great. There are swords all over this planet and must be millions more on the other worlds." I knew Chopper was better than any Earth-made sword without magic, but magic was as common as allergies on the other worlds. It couldn't possibly be that rare. Maybe he was stuck here on Earth for now, and there weren't that many other magical swords around.

He curled a pale lip. "If you believe that, you are more ignorant than I thought."

The magical tiger disappeared from my awareness, his aura vanishing. What the hell? He'd been up near the tower the last time I'd checked on him.

I couldn't tell if the cub had also disappeared. Her aura had been weak, too weak for me to detect from the grand hall.

"Drop the sword, or I will kill him," the vampire stated.

I was so close to sawing through the bar. But what then? Even if I kicked it free and could get out, I would still have to face the wizard, the vampire, and those wolves.

"I already gave you my deal," I said.

"Unacceptable."

His fingers tightened, and Michael gasped in pain, his back arching as magic flowed down his spine.

If I'd thought the vampire was bluffing, I might have been able to hold out, might have been able to do nothing while my friend writhed in pain. But the vampire's icy eyes said he would kill Michael and then send his wizard and wolves in to take the sword from me. And they could do it. Even if Willard had still been here, we couldn't have fought off two powerful magic users. I certainly couldn't by myself, especially when that tiger might reappear at any moment. I was surprised the vampire didn't already realize he had me overpowered and that he could easily force the issue. Maybe he thought the sword was more powerful than it was.

Michael dropped to his knees. Blood ran out of his left ear and dripped off his stubbled jaw.

"Fine," I called. "Stop."

I turned the sword, so I could stick it out through the gap and prepare to drop it.

The vampire released Michael, who dropped to his hands and knees, still gasping, but more in relief now than pain. The magic that had been flowing into him ceased.

"I'm sorry, Val," he rasped, looking up at me.

"It's not your fault. It's mine. I'm sorry this asshole dragged you up here."

"I know you are." Michael managed a quick smile. "If there was anything to forgive, I would forgive you."

The vampire's eyes narrowed, and he lifted a warning hand toward Michael.

"Let him come over here, and I'll drop the sword." I still held Chopper out of the cage but hadn't yet let go.

"Drop it now, or I'll finish what I started." The vampire drew a magical bone dagger from a belt sheath, the wicked blade almost a foot long. He held it over Michael's back.

I shook my head. "I want him out of your range before—"

A blast of magical power struck my wrist like a sledgehammer. Chopper tumbled from my grip and clanged to the floor. The ogre sneered and twitched the end of his staff. My sword levitated four feet into the air and floated toward the vampire.

I swore and brought up Fezzik, but the ogre hurled another blast of power toward me, this time at the cage instead of my wrist. The vampire lunged at Michael, that bone dagger raised. I fired at him through the bars, but the ogre's attack landed, and my cage rocked wildly. The dagger plunged through Michael's spine, and he screamed.

"No!" I screamed just as loudly, feeling as if the blade had plunged into my own heart.

The chain holding the cage, the chain Willard had weakened with her shots, snapped. I plummeted to the floor.

"Kill her," the vampire said, snatching Chopper out of the air and striding for the back hallway.

The cage landed sideways, the bar I'd been sawing now above me. I twisted onto my back and kicked at it.

Snaps and snarls sounded as the wolves ran toward me. Even worse, the aura of the tiger reappeared, right at the ogre's side.

A part of me wanted to stay in the cage and hope the animals couldn't get at me, but there would be no safety in that. The ogre would hurl magic to kill me as I lay helplessly pinned.

I kicked again and again. The bar snapped, flying upward. I squeezed through the gap, hefted Fezzik, and sprayed fire at the oncoming wolves, at the tiger loping behind them, and at the ogre. He leveled his staff at me again, and I knew my death was inevitable. Michael lay crumpled on the floor where the vampire had left him, blood pooled under his unmoving body, and I feared he was already dead.

The tiger's eyes met mine as I tried to shoot at all the animals surging toward me. I couldn't read anything in them, and when he sprang, his powerful muscles taking him past the wolves, I was certain he was eager to reach me first.

But the tiger landed and snapped his great jaws to the left and to the right, tearing out the throats of the two wolves closest to him.

I was so startled that I stopped firing for a second. But more wolves were coming—they were almost upon me. I focused on the ones that weren't near the tiger and that hadn't yet noticed he'd turned on them. The wolves had eyes only for me.

The ogre shouted, "Stop!" in his own language.

The tiger froze, halted by the magical command. My bullets took one wolf in the eye, and it toppled to the ground. Another one leaped, springing for the cage I was still halfway inside of. I hit it twice, once in each of its eyes, my magical bullets gouging into its brain.

That was the last of the wolves, and just as I thought I might survive, a blast of power from the ogre hit me square in the chest.

It tore me out of the cage and hurled me all the way to the wall. I slammed into it like a human wrecking ball, wood splintering all around me. The blow knocked all the air out of my lungs and made my entire chest spasm as I tumbled to the floor, Fezzik falling from my grip.

The tiger prowled toward me. Not in mighty leaps and bounds, but slowly, a cat stalking his prey.

Or maybe not quite that. His eyes were hard to read, but the ogre kept chanting something. An order to kill me, not a spell. The tiger had no choice but to obey.

The blow had shocked my solar plexus, and I couldn't breathe, but I lunged and snatched Fezzik again. I turned the weapon not on the tiger, who was less than ten feet away, but toward the ogre. And held down the trigger, willing every bullet to slam into his chest.

But the ogre saw the attack coming and, with a whisper of magic, formed an invisible shield in front of himself. My bullets ricocheted away, embedding in the ceiling and the walls.

The tiger crouched to spring. Reluctantly, I turned my weapon toward him.

Then gunfire rang out, not from me but from the other end of the grand hall. Willard had stepped inside from behind, her rifle on auto as she rained bullets into the ogre's unprotected back. She'd found a way to sneak around, and thanks to her lack of magical blood and lack of a magical weapon, the ogre hadn't sensed her coming. And his shield didn't extend around to his back.

The rounds pounded into him. They weren't magical, but they were effective.

He lost his concentration, and his defenses dropped. I skittered to the side so Willard wouldn't be in my sights if I missed, and joined her in firing at the sturdy ogre. Bullets pummeled him from both sides, and his staff clattered to the floor. I finally managed to gasp in a few stuttered breaths as he pitched over sideways next to it.

The tiger was still in his crouch, poised to spring at me, but for whatever reason, he hadn't attacked. He looked back at the ogre, and when the wizard's aura faded, his life disappearing from his body, the tiger disappeared from our world.

Willard stopped firing, and I sprinted around the cage and the dead wolves to fall to my knees beside Michael. Hoping in vain, I touched shaking fingers to his throat. But the vampire was an expert at death, and he'd succeeded at killing my best friend.

Only the knowledge that the vampire was still on the loose—and with my sword, damn it—kept me from breaking down.

"Fuck," Willard said, slumping against the doorjamb. "Nothing in this place dies like it should."

She was glaring at the ogre, dozens of bullets riddling his body.

"Only mere humans," I whispered, stroking the side of Michael's head, tears threatening even though I couldn't relax yet, couldn't let myself fall apart.

"He didn't make it?" Willard hadn't been here. She hadn't seen the vampire's fatal blow.

"No." I forced myself to stand and take a deep breath, hoping to steady myself, though my entire body quivered with rage. I was going to find that bastard, yank my sword out of his hands, and use it to kill him.

"I'm sorry. I attacked that elf when I ran across him back in that maze—" Willard tilted her head toward the hallway she'd come from, "—but he hurled me against a wall with the power of a Mack truck and disappeared into his warren."

Only then did I realize that the side of Willard's face was bloody, and she gripped her ribs with one hand as she held her rifle with the other, her finger on the trigger as she glared into the dark hallway.

"He's got my sword," I said.

"I saw. Can it kill a vampire?"

"If I cleave off his head. And I'll have zero trouble doing that right now." With the rage coursing through my limbs, I could have beheaded an army of vampires.

"We'll go after him. He's a murderer and needs to be stopped." Willard turned to head deeper into the castle.

"Wait." I dashed tears out of my eyes, stalked to the ogre's body, and ripped the chain with the cat charm off his neck. Though I had no idea how it worked, I was positive it was what summoned and controlled the big tiger. "We're not running around back there and stumbling into the devil knows how many more traps are littering this place."

"Can you sense him? Did he leave the castle?"

"I can, and he's still here. He's in an underground level somewhere, toward the back."

"What's the plan then?" Willard, dashing away the blood on her face, looked ready to stomp back there and find him, but she waited.

I grabbed one of the lanterns off the wall. "We get Michael's body out of here, get the cub out of the tower if she's still there, then burn this hellhole to the ground so that coward has to come out and face us in the daylight."

"I don't think the amount of daylight out there visible through that fog is going to kill him," Willard said, but she ran around the room, snatching lanterns from the walls.

"Maybe not, but *I'll* do that."

CHAPTER 18

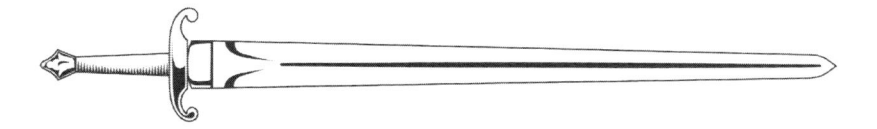

I'D FAILED AND MICHAEL WAS dead.

From the trees around the burning castle, I hurled another grenade over the high walls and onto the rooftop. It exploded with a thunderous boom that shook the earth but did nothing to alleviate my anger. Anger with the situation and anger with myself. I'd expected traps, and I'd *still* managed to walk into one.

I grabbed another grenade and pulled the pin.

The log structure burned heartily from all sides, the flames writhing in the weak morning light, blurred and surreal in the omnipresent fog. The water in the moat reflected the hazy orange of the fire. When the grenades blew, they added carnage to the slaughterhouse, but they weren't needed. Willard and I had doused numerous halls and rooms in kerosene from the lanterns, lighting carpets and tapestries and furnishings with the dedication of revenge-fueled arsonists.

The tower where the cub had been was burning like a candle. When we'd checked, she hadn't been in there. Hopefully, the big tiger had taken her someplace safe, but it further distressed me, knowing I would never see her again.

Everything about this morning was abysmal. I threw another grenade.

Two of the alligators in the moat scurried up onto land. At first, I thought they were being magically compelled to attack us, but they rushed toward the woods. They were fleeing the flames, not doing the vampire's bidding. But he still had some of those wolves with him. I sensed their auras down in a basement, just as I sensed his.

"Has he moved yet?" Willard asked over the snapping and cracking of wood.

She stood behind me, rifle at the ready and eyes alert as she scanned the hilltop.

"He's still underground back there." I waved toward the rear of the burning castle, a portion we hadn't seen yet. We had stationed ourselves to the side of the structure so we would see if he came out of either the front or back.

"He could have a fire-proof saferoom."

"If he does, we'll find it once the castle burns to the ground." I squeezed my hand around the haft of a great axe I'd removed from one of the walls inside. It wasn't Chopper by any stretch of the imagination, but a hint of magic imbued the blade. It might work to behead the vampire if I could get close enough to him.

"We should split up so we can cover both exits in case he runs."

"I already have a plan for if he runs." I held up the cat charm I'd taken from the ogre.

Willard arched her eyebrows. "Pretty."

"It summons the tiger."

"Do we want that?"

"Yes." I hoped.

I also hoped I could get the charm to work. I hadn't seen the ogre mutter an activation word to call forth the tiger.

Gripping the charm in my hand, I whispered, "Come back to this realm, my friend."

Willard must have caught the words over the roar of the fire, or was a gifted lip reader, because her eyebrows flew up again. There was little doubt that the tiger had been responsible for the slayings of the past week, including that of her agent, but if my guess was right, he couldn't act of his own volition. He'd been forced by magic to do as the ogre wished, the ogre who'd been obediently serving the vampire.

"Come back, tiger," I whispered, worried when nothing happened. Maybe I had to know his name to summon him.

The aura I'd been monitoring for the last twenty minutes stirred. The vampire was on the move.

I pointed toward the castle's back door—he was heading in that direction. Willard and I would have to chase after him ourselves.

"He's going for that door." As I started in that direction, a silver mist formed. The tiger.

I shifted the big axe into both hands in case I was wrong about the figurine and he attacked me.

Willard jogged off, not waiting to see the creature solidifying in the mist.

"The wolves are coming with him," I called after her, intending to follow as soon as the tiger fully formed.

"Good. I can kill *them* with this." She hefted her mundane rifle as she ran.

I almost yelled a reminder that only shots directly to the eye had worked before, but she knew that. And could do that.

The tiger solidified in front of me, his head as high as my shoulder as he stood on all fours.

"I need your help." I squeezed the cat figurine, clenching against the shaft of the axe. "Will you chase down the vampire and hold him down so I can kill him? Permanently?"

Unwavering green eyes stared at me. He had to understand—he'd run off to find the cub when I'd told him about her—but could he communicate? And would he be willing to do what I asked? Or did I have to make it an order?

You retrieved the cub, he spoke telepathically into my mind.

"Yeah."

Gunshots rang out. The wolves had run out the back gate ahead of the vampire, and Willard was firing at them as they leaped over the moat. I had to get over there to help her, but the tiger would improve our odds vastly.

And cared for her, he said.

"I tried. She wouldn't eat or drink."

Our kind cannot do so in this world. I thought she would die because she had no statuette, no link back to Del'noth. The tiger gazed past my shoulder toward the wolves and toward Willard firing at them from the cover of a tree.

"Will you help us?" I hated to rush his story, but the vampire wouldn't give us time for a long tête-à-tête.

I was the one who took her from her mother, compelled to do so by the ogre. His gaze returned to mine. *To be used as bait for your treasure-hunter acquaintance to find.*

"Yeah, they screwed us all over. Come help me deal with the vampire, eh?" More gunshots fired, and I couldn't wait any longer for the tiger to decide if he was going to help. Maybe a sterner order would have compelled him to obey, but the last thing I wanted was for that to backfire and for him to attack *me*.

As I rushed across the hilltop between the trees and the moat, coughing at the smoke curling down my throat and dodging charred pieces of wood blowing off the castle, the vampire stepped into view. He focused on Willard. Chopper rested on his shoulder, but it was an empty hand he stretched toward her.

I wasn't close enough to use the axe, so I yanked out Fezzik. He hurled his power at Willard an instant before I fired, and she flew backward, smashing into a tree. Two out of four wolves remained on their feet, and they charged toward her.

My bullets pounded into the vampire's side under his raised arm. He jerked it down and faced me. I fired into his chest. The rounds struck true, but he had no blood to bleed, no organs to destroy. Even magical bullets weren't enough to blow away a vampire.

He squinted at me, and I braced myself for an attack, but when he raised his hand, it was to form a shimmering silver circle that hung perpendicular to the earth. A portal. I'd never seen one, but I knew from stories told by the magical what they looked like. He intended to escape—with my sword.

I roared and ran at him, firing. He turned for the portal, and I knew I wouldn't reach him in time.

My clip ran empty, and I almost threw my trusty firearm at the vampire in frustration—and in the vain hope that he would trip over it and go down. Then a blur of silver blasted past me. The tiger.

He slammed into our foe like a pile driver, and Chopper flew out of the vampire's hands as they tumbled to the ground. I cast aside the axe and sprinted for my sword as the snarls and snapping of jaws rose over the crackling fire. Whether the tiger's claws could destroy a vampire, I didn't know, but I snatched up Chopper to help.

They rolled on the ground, and I couldn't get in to strike at the vampire without the risk of hurting the tiger. Then a blast of magical power struck my ally in the chest. He flew backward as if he weighed ten pounds instead of a thousand.

The vampire, elf that he was, sprang lithely to his feet, but I was ready and so was Chopper. The blade flared blue in the smoky haze as I swept it toward him. He ducked but not fast enough. Chopper crashed into the side of his head, splitting his skull.

But he felt no pain, and crackling power struck me like lightning. I gasped and stumbled back, almost losing my grip on the sword. But I tightened my hands around the hilt, refusing to lose it again.

Gunfire echoed to the side, Willard dealing with the rest of the wolves.

The tiger launched himself into the vampire again, claws raking him with deadly fury. The magic assaulting me disappeared, and I rushed in, determined to take advantage.

Another burst of power flowed from the vampire, knocking the tiger back. This time, I sprang in before the vampire could leap to his feet again. I caught him halfway up and swung my blade like an executioner's axe. The sword flared brighter than ever and cut through the vampire's neck like it was butter.

The head flew off, rolling across the ashy earth until it bumped to a stop under the portal. With the vampire no longer controlling it, that portal winked out.

The gunfire stopped, and I picked out Willard among the trees, still standing. She walked out toward me. Toward *us*.

With the vampire dead—truly dead—the tiger sat and looked toward the burning castle. Thinking of his former... owner? Master? I didn't know how the charm worked and couldn't guess how long he'd been bound to the ogre, but I doubted he'd liked his time spent with him. Would he try to take the charm from me now to gain his freedom? Was that possible?

"Thank you for the help," I told him.

He gazed at me with his green eyes, his silver fur glowing in the fog, then disappeared from our world and from my senses.

Willard lifted her phone as she approached. "Captain Rodriguez texted. He's wrapped up and is on his way to help us carry out the body."

The body. Michael. I closed my eyes again, distressed anew at the reminder that this was real, that I hadn't gotten here in time to save him.

"Thanks," I made myself say.

"You're welcome." Willard looked at the burning castle. "This is going to be a bitch of a report to write up."

And what would that report say? That all of this—all of the deaths—had been because some kooky vampire had wanted my sword?

I gazed down at the blade. I would have given it up to have Michael back.

EPILOGUE

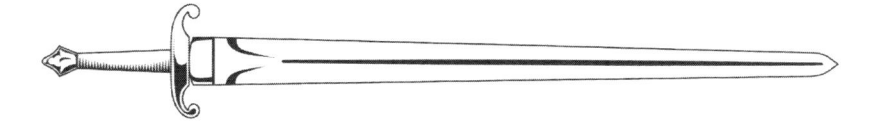

I PARKED ALONG THE STREET IN front of Willard's building and debated if I could summon the fortitude to go inside. While I'd been at Michael's funeral, she'd texted that she wanted to talk to me, no hint of what about.

Given everything that had happened in Bellingham, from Michael's death to innocent people being killed by the tiger I could now summon, she might want to press charges against me. Or order me to leave the city and never return.

Julie had more or less requested that. Even though they didn't know the full truth about what had happened, Michael's family had been flinty to me at the funeral. I'd spent most of it standing in the rain under an umbrella, feeling lonelier than I'd ever been and like more of a failure than I'd ever been. I didn't know if I needed a long vacation, where I'd try to forget everything that had happened this month, or a new job to distract me from it all. It was possible neither would work.

Not bothering with an umbrella, I let the rain hit me on the head as I walked inside. Willard was in her office. She still didn't have an assistant for the outer desk.

As I stepped inside, I looked warily around for police officers prepared to step out and cuff me. But she was the only one there, sitting behind her desk and typing on the computer. A manila folder rested on the corner next to an enormous cup of coffee. Rainwater slithered down the back of my neck.

"Hey," I said warily.

"*Hey?*" Her eyebrows rose. "You'd think someone who was in the military for ten years would address an officer by rank."

"You used my grenades. I thought we were friends now."

"I am your potential employer debating on offering you a contract." Willard pressed a finger to the folder.

"Oh? I thought you might have called me in to have me arrested."

"Have you committed a crime?"

"I am the reason crimes have been committed."

"Then maybe you should renew your devotion to tracking down criminals who've raped, killed, and plundered. Some people need to walk in the dark, so others can live in the light. You seem to get that."

"Yeah. I do."

She tapped the folder. "I'm authorized to pay you what Hobbs paid you. You interested?"

"Yes." I gazed at the folder without stepping forward, half-expecting another trap to spring. It wasn't as if I'd done anything that should have changed Willard's opinion of me. If anything, she ought to think I was more of a loose cannon than before. The only good thing that had come out of our adventure was that the vampire was dead, and the tiger was in the hands of someone who wouldn't send him out to kill innocent people. "What's changed?"

"When we first met, I thought you were a reckless vigilante and a sarcastic smartass who would be obnoxious to work with."

"And now?"

"Now I'm sure of it."

I snorted. "Great."

"I'm still going to offer you work when I have it, because you're good at what you do, you're decked out like a battleship, and I think you care about doing the right thing."

"I do."

"Good."

I stepped forward and picked up the folder. No traps sprang. I guess

I shouldn't have expected them. Willard had helped me out of a trap, not driven me into one.

"I'm sorry I didn't get around behind them in time to stop them from killing your friend," she said, her voice softening.

"Thanks," I rasped, emotion forming a knot in my throat. "The funeral sucked."

"They usually do." She stuck out her fist, and I remembered my joke about fist bumps.

We cracked knuckles, and I walked out with the folder under my arm. The rain had stopped, and the sun peeked through the clouds. It seemed like the first time in ages that it hadn't been foggy or rainy. It wasn't enough to lift my spirits, and I would regret Michael's death for a long time, but at least I had a job and a path forward.

When I reached the Jeep, I read the file, then touched the new feline-shaped charm around my neck and summoned the big silver tiger.

Mist formed at my side, and he coalesced in it, the green eyes that gazed at me statelier than those of the cub, but similar in many ways.

"I've got a mission to track down some orcs who are stealing people from a corn maze out in Snohomish and ransoming them to their families for money—and killing them if the ransoms aren't paid." I opened the door, put the seats down because he looked far too huge to sit on them, and stepped aside. "You interested in hunting them down?"

You possess my figurine now. You can command me to do whatever you wish.

"I'd rather have a willing partner who does what *he* wishes."

He gazed at me, and I expected him to tell me he wished to be left alone.

"I'm going to be working on saving people's lives and killing bad guys going forward. Atoning for my sins or something. I thought you might be interested in doing the same." I arched my eyebrows. I'd gotten the impression that he hadn't been pleased to be used by the ogre and the vampire.

He regarded me for a long minute, then sprang into the Jeep, crouching low to keep his head from hitting the ceiling. *I will accompany you.*

"Good." I went around to the driver's seat, then laughed because I couldn't see anything out the rearview mirror. He was bigger than a dog. A *lot* bigger. "Is the cub doing okay? Did you take her back to her mother?"

Yes. She is well. Her mother was pleased at her safe return and very angry at me for having taken her.

"Will she forgive you?"

Perhaps in time. Not all of my kind are bound by statuettes, but enough are that all understand. The tiger tilted his big silver head. *The mother was perplexed that the cub returned with a gray fabric band in her mouth.*

"That's probably the piece of my seatbelt she chewed off when I wasn't looking." Impressive that she'd taken it with her. "I hope she appreciates the memento."

When last I saw her, she was using it for a tug game with her siblings.

I smiled, sad that she was gone but glad she had gotten to go back to her normal life and her family.

The tiger's nostrils twitched. *Your conveyance smells abysmal.*

"Willard said it stunk back there, so I got this at the car wash." I pointed at a yellow pine-tree air freshener dangling from the rearview mirror. "It's Vanillaroma."

It's unacceptable.

"The other option is…" I fished in the glove compartment and pulled out a blue tree still in the wrapper. "Caribbean Colada."

Dreadful. I can smell it through the plastic.

"Look, tiger, atonement isn't easy." I turned the key in the ignition. "If you want, I can stop and get you some cotton balls to stuff in your nostrils."

My name is Sindari Dargoth Chaser the Third, Son of the Chieftain Raul, Feared Stalker and Hunter of the Tangled Tundra Nation on Del'noth.

I was about to say I was honored that he'd given me his name, but he wrinkled his nose, reached over with his paw, and pressed the button for the automatic window. He stuck his head out and made a gagging noise. It seemed I'd gotten a magical tiger with a flair for melodrama.

"Can I call you Sindari?"

Yes.

"I'm Val."

Take us to the orcs, Val. I will instruct you on how to insert small dreadfully scented trees into their nostrils.

"That should defeat them handily."

I have no doubt.

THE END